ONE TRUTH

An Exciting Story with Spiritual Insight

Book Two

JASON M. JOLIN

WESTBOW
PRESS®
A DIVISION OF THOMAS NELSON
& ZONDERVAN

WestBow Press books may be ordered through booksellers or by contacting:

WestBow Press
A Division of Thomas Nelson & Zondervan
1663 Liberty Drive
Bloomington, IN 47403
www.westbowpress.com
844-714-3454

Scripture quotations are taken from the (NASB®) New American Standard
Bible®, Copyright © 1960, 1971, 1977, 1995, 2020 by The Lockman
Foundation. Used by permission. All rights reserved. lockman.org.

ISBN: 979-8-3850-3989-0 (sc)
ISBN: 979-8-3850-3990-6 (e)

Library of Congress Control Number: 2024926402

Print information available on the last page.

WestBow Press rev. date: 02/05/2025

ACKNOWLEDGMENTS

I dedicate this book to my amazing wife, Kristina Jolin. She has helped me with all my books, including this one, currently her favorite. I am so thankful for her reading my drafts and answering numerous questions, without ever complaining; and she was influential in my choosing a 1st person point-of-view. I also very much appreciate all her support with our family that enabled me to write this book – she is an amazing mother to our children. I am truly blessed to have her as my wife.

I also want to thank Ron Cook, a member of my church, for continuously encouraging me to write this sequel. It's a reminder to all of us that words of encouragement can have a big impact on others.

I pray that my children, Trevor, Toriana, Titus and Addilyn will love God with all their heart, soul and mind, and always seek to follow truth.

Most of all, I want to thank God for enabling me to write this book. My hope is that it is helpful for those seeking spiritual truth.

INTRODUCTION

"I want the truth!"

"You can't handle the truth!"

These are the most famous quotes from the movie: *A Few Good Men*[1]; and I want to use them to introduce the purpose of this book. In certain ways, they relate to concerns I have for millions of souls.

Let's start with the first quote. For those who saw the movie, you'll recall the scene: Lieutenant Kaffee (played by Tom Cruise) is questioning Colonel Jessup (played by Jack Nicholson) in a courtroom about the death of a U.S. marine. Kaffee knows that grilling a Colonel in an accusatory manner could lead to serious trouble for him personally, but he decides he wants the truth, regardless of the cost. He yells at Jessup, "I want the truth!"

When it comes to religion, do people want the truth? Unfortunately, many people are apathetic. They don't really care about spiritual truth. Some go through the motions of their religious upbringing, but it's a low priority. Others don't consider religion at all; instead, they're focused exclusively on this world.

I'm astounded by this mindset. While life is important, we will die someday. We don't know when, but it's a fact that will happen to all of us. Given what is at stake – *where we spend eternity* – we should all *want to know the truth about God*; and, like Kaffee, pursue it with passion!

Second, notice that Kaffee says he wants <u>the</u> truth. Not <u>a</u> truth. He is not after someone's subjective opinion. No – there is one objective truth regarding what happened to the dead soldier in the movie. Similarly, there is one truth about God. Since major religions have core beliefs that contradict, it's logically impossible that they are all true. In fact, Jesus made a direct claim refuting the idea of multiple truths; in the Bible verse below, He claimed to be _the truth_ and the only way to heaven:

> Jesus said to him, "I am the way, and _the truth_, and the life; _no one comes to the Father except through Me_. (John 14:6 NASB emphasis added)

While it might sound nice to say everyone's religious view is valid, it is not possible to have multiple truths about God. It is a dangerous lie I will discuss in this book.

For my third point, let's consider the second quote. Jessup fires back at Kaffee telling him he can't handle the truth. When it comes to religion, many people can't handle seeking spiritual truth. They let their preferences influence their beliefs. They follow what seems interesting or feels good.

But holding to an untrue belief about God is dangerous because it can lead to a false sense of security about the judgment we all face. How important is truth? It is one reason God came to Earth as a human (Jesus claimed to be God and proved He is God). Consider what Jesus said when He was being questioned by the Roman Governor Pontius Pilate.

> Therefore Pilate said to Him, "So You are a king?" Jesus answered, "You say correctly that I am a king. _For this purpose I have been born, and for this I have come into the world: to testify to the truth._ Everyone who is of the truth listens to My voice." (John 18:37 NASB emphasis added).

Jesus said He came to testify to the truth.[2] Obviously truth is essential. If it is important to Him, it should be important to us.

But it's not enough to simply care about the spiritual truth, recognize there is one truth about God, and be open to discovering it. Can we truly handle the truth? Handling the truth implies action; and that is what all of us need to consider once we know the truth – we need to commit to it!

When it comes to life on Earth, we all care very much about truth. We want our family and friends to be honest with us. We want our doctor to tell us the truth. We demand the truth from any expert we pay – accountant, lawyer, electrician, etc. We want all of them to tell us the truth, not what they think we want to hear. How much more important is the truth that determines the destination of our soul?

The purpose of this book is to share important principles regarding spiritual truth. It is book two of a trilogy. The first book, *One Fear*, was about a father helping his children survive, while also teaching them reasons to believe Christianity is true. This book picks up where *One Fear* left off, from a third-person point of view; but transitions to first-person as Lucy shares what happened in Brazil, and this point-of-view continues for the remainder of the book. While the story and its characters are fictional, the evidence and principles of truth that are discussed are non-fiction. It is known as Christian apologetics. There is a summary of key points related to the topic of truth at the end of the book.

Let's begin.

CHAPTER
ONE

"Come on Zach," Lucy hollers up the stairs. "We can't be late."

Currently they have plenty of time to get to where they're headed, but Lucy doesn't want to be in a rush outdoors. That's the surest way to miss an obvious danger. To walk into peril that could have been avoided, but instead ends your life. Slow and careful has kept them alive; and she wants extra time to get to the location where she is leading a critical meeting. She summoned eleven families with a simple note:

Urgent Meeting. Saturday 10 am. Baxter's Football Field. God Bless, Lucy.

Lucy walks back into the kitchen to finish filling a backpack with food and a few survival items. They shouldn't need matches, medical supplies, extra ammunition or a solar-powered flashlight; but she doesn't travel far from home without them, just in case. After she finishes packing some food, she reaches for a loaded handgun, checks the safety mechanism and tucks it into the back of her jeans.

Lucy is nervous. There's a lot at stake today. She can actually feel the jitters in her limbs. This is unlike her. Usually she is calm, and confident, even in this harsh world. But today could change the course of their lives.

Zach lumbers down the steps of their two-story home. He is not in his typical chipper mood. "When will we get back?" he asks in the exasperated, winey tone of an eight-year-old.

"Hopefully a few hours," Lucy responds as she snaps a latch on the backpack. "Maybe a little longer." She glances over and notices his glum demeanor.

"Can't I just stay here? Nobody ever comes around."

"Zachary." She tilts her head and gives him a disapproving frown. "We've talked about this before. It's just too dangerous." She pauses, not wanting to elaborate on the newest threat that terrifies her, even though he will hear it later today. The world is beyond harsh. Almost unfathomable.

The human population has been decimated by D6, a fatal muscular disease. The first wave of D6 ended seventeen years ago, after the annihilation of Australia. But a second wave emerged two years later, terrorizing the world. It took the lives of billions. Eventually, with enough quarantining, the virus that causes D6 faded, and those who survived started to rebuild the world.

It all went away for eight years, and Lucy thought the nightmare was over, but the third wave – known as D63 – struck with a vengeance. Similar to the original virus, it causes a disease in the human body that randomly attacks muscles, stretching them to the point of tearing, rendering them useless. The pain is excruciating. When the random attacks eventually strike a vital organ, such as the heart, the person succumbs to death. It is highly contagious and swept through the world. It devastated every civilization, leaving behind only small fragments of humanity.

There are rumors of larger populations living with strict sanitation rules; but so far, none of these have been found to be credible from the sources Lucy has contacted.

Most people live in isolation, but some have formed what is known as communities – small groups, usually twenty people or less – that live in a close vicinity. They share critical resources needed to survive, while having minimal contact. Some communities accept more interaction between members beyond their household; only if they trust people to be candid about potential infection.

Being honest about possible exposure is even more important now. D63 is unique and more dangerous because this wave has migrated to the animal kingdom.

Cold-blooded creatures on land became carriers; but, while this variant among insects and reptiles can spread between animals, it doesn't infect humans. Unfortunately, warm-blooded mammals have a mutated strain that can spread to humans through bodily fluids. Even domestic animals became carriers. People living in isolation were no longer safe.

No one knows exactly how animals acquired the virus, but two theories emerged. One is it came from carnivorous animals feeding on human corpses, somehow digesting and surviving the virus. As they were then bitten by mosquitos and ticks, the virus quickly transmitted to other animals. The alternative theory is it started with organisms involved with the decomposition of dead bodies – particularly flies and beetles. These critters were then eaten by other animals farther up the food chain, and this continued until all animals were infected. The latter theory is considered more plausible.

Ironically, D63 is only harmful to humans, which perplexed medical experts. Before the scientific community dissipated, they theorized it is because of humankind's unique DNA structure. It's unclear if D63 has migrated to sea creatures, but Lucy assumes it has, just to be safe.

As the human population has dwindled, the animal kingdom has expanded, overtaking all environments. Overpopulation of mammals is rampant. It's not uncommon to hear coyotes, see wolves searching for prey, or witness predators battle for a meal, which all serve as a reminder of the risk of ambush. Any human coming in contact with fluids of a mammal carrying D63, such as through bites, is likely to be infected.

All that said, the new danger Zach has yet to hear about, scares Lucy more than the disease.

Lucy reaches over and messes up Zach's hair. "We'll be back soon and have something fun for dinner."

Fun is hard to come by. Food sources are primarily plants they grow, livestock they raise and mammals they hunt. Eggs are typical in the morning, and chicken or some other animal protein is common for dinner. As long as animal food sources are cooked, there's no fear of contracting D63. It's a painstaking process to carefully kill and clean mammals for food with gloves and a mask; but most survivors have gotten used to it. Fun food means Lucy will try to find something unique in the limited variety they have.

Zach doesn't look interested.

"I'll see if I can make a sugary treat," Lucy offers. Candy and packaged snacks are long gone, either eaten or spoiled; but they have several containers of honey. She mixes fruit with honey when they desire a sweet delicacy.

He smirks, and she decides that's the best reaction she's going to get.

Lucy throws her backpack over her right shoulder and grabs a rifle, while Zach finishes tying his sneakers. She then fastens the makeshift, light armor they created around both of Zach's shins, over his jeans, to protect against a surprise animal attack. She follows that by attaching light armor to his forearms. While they don't protect the entire body, they offer some defense for areas likely to be bitten. Lucy has already attached similar armor to herself. She nods approval to open the door and exit.

They leave the house through the front door. Lucy pauses to check the surroundings before locking up.

As usual, the suburban neighborhood is quiet. Houses are spaced apart in lot sizes of a few acres. Foliage overgrowth dominates the environment. But in reality, it's especially silent because most people are gone. Over 99% of the world's population has succumbed to multiple waves of D6.

Lucy turns the deadbolt, locking the front door. A small obstacle to impede strangers from raiding their home, which is very unlikely, but it's still a habit for her. She scans the environment looking for immediate danger. Nothing apparent. The temperature is cool, as the nighttime chill has lingered. Frost on the grass is a reminder it is late Fall. Lucy dreads the winter. Keeping a fire going for warmth is a lot of work.

"Let's go Zach." Lucy's left hand gently nudges his back toward a stack of twelve, small orange cones. "Can you grab those cones? I need you to carry them to the field."

"Too heavyyyyy." Zach jokes, as he fakes not being able to lift them off the ground.

"Ha!" Lucy says with a smile. "You're funny." She is genuinely thankful her son has kept his sense of humor in spite of the cruel world in which they live. He picks up the cones and they're on their way.

They make their way to the road by way of the cracked driveway, choosing to avoid the long grass in the front yard. Their house is the middle of three houses at the end of a cul-de-sac. It's a long-straight road ahead of them, with five houses on either side, before connecting to one of the main roads in this rural town.

As they progress, trees and thick bushes bracket them on either side of the road. Long grass dominates what was once front lawns. The morning sun delivers rays of light through the foliage to the left and birds chatter in the trees. Lucy would delight in a day such as this, if there were no need to worry about a deadly virus lurking in the world, moving amongst host animals. Lucy tries to enjoy small bits of pleasure, while still being vigilant.

As they walk along the road, Zach kicks a rock ahead of his path. Years of weather has broken up the once smooth asphalt, leaving behind small chunks of tar. Patches of grass have emerged in the craters of the broken road. The street gives the appearance of a warzone.

Lucy's eyes continuously scan the foliage on either side, looking for the slightest hint of danger. Listening for any indication that a dangerous mammal is stalking them. Because humanity is so sparse, this new world is dominated by plants and animals.

Dangerous mammals are the biggest concern. Grizzly bears are the most powerful, and if they surprise someone, they could end the person's life quickly with their strength and sharp claws. Wolverines and fisher cats are vicious, but fortunately they usually hunt at night, and typically leave humans alone unless cornered or surprised. Lucy has seen a few during the day, perhaps too hungry to wait until darkness. They make nighttime travel treacherous. But she is currently most worried about wolves, which hunt in packs and are more difficult to fend off with one gun. Although they typically hunt during dusk or dawn, she has seen them frequently in daylight.

"Mom?" Zach startles her concentration. "Last night you said you would tell me how you made it home from Brazil."

"Later Zach," she says abruptly, continuing to scan and listen as they proceed.

A minute later, she glances over at her son, whose head has dropped. He has stopped kicking a rock, and simply shuffles along in obvious disappointment. It tugs at her heart, but Lucy feels she needs to stay alert. A lack of focus is the surest way to be ambushed.

"You said you would," Zach mutters.

Lucy presses her lips and frowns. His disappointment on what is a small request makes her reconsider. "If there is time when we get to the football field, then I will tell you. But not now. You know I need to stay alert."

Zach's demeanor changes instantly, and he selects a new rock to kick along the road.

To their left is Tabitha's house. She was Lucy's best friend; but unfortunately, they lost the close connection they had after the tragedy that took the life of Tabitha's mom.

Lucy looks over to her right, at the porch of a neighbor's house they're currently walking by. It has a chair blocking the front door, a sign that at least one person in the house had the disease and no one should enter. It was the universal signal around the world of an infected home. Any entrance blocked by a chair meant 'stay out.'

They pass a couple more houses that have neighbors whom Lucy also expects to see, but the majority of homes are vacant. There are no signs of human life. Lucy hears a couple birds chirping loudly and then a dog bark in the distance. The only other sound is rustling leaves on the trees, caused by an occasional breeze.

They reach the end of their road and turn right onto a main street that connects multiple developments. They follow this street for over thirty minutes, taking them past town hall and other buildings that have become a wasteland. Eventually, they turn off on a side road heading toward the high school football field, with vacant houses on either side.

Lucy hears the crunch of sand under her boots as they proceed. The quietness of the neighborhood catches her attention. It's eerie. Unlike her son, she remembers a time when this area was alive with the sounds of civilization. But now, the vast majority of the homes in the neighborhood are void of human life. She yearns for the days of her youth.

Eventually they reach an opening in a chain-linked fence at the end of the road. It leads to the back of the football field – the location of their meeting. It is outdoors and spacious, alleviating fears of breathing the same air of other people, while also offering protection against animal predators.

Lucy is extra cautious at this opening, as bushes and trees on either side are much closer; thankfully there doesn't seem to be any detectable danger. A narrow rocky path that cuts through long grass, about knee-high, leads toward the football field.

Lucy cautiously proceeds through the fence and toward the field, with Zach behind her. She lowers her rifle and swings it left and right, carefully scanning the grass for small but vicious mammals, like a fisher cat. A surprise discovery could lead to a fatal bite. Zach follows her path.

Lucy stops suddenly and swings her left arm back to stop Zach.

"What?" he asks, with a mix of fear and curiosity.

Lucy thought she saw movement in the grass directly ahead, just off the path; but she doesn't respond to her son yet. She studies the area, trying to determine if there's a threat.

"What is it?" he inquires again, this time in a whisper.

"Wait," she responds.

Lucy doesn't see any more movement. She wonders if it was her imagination.

Lucy takes a step forward and reaches her rifle toward the area to push the long grass to the side. Clearing some grass reveals a large snake in a coiled position. It looks like a rattlesnake with the head of some kind of vermin in its mouth that it must have recently captured.

Lucy considers what might have happened if they were just a few minutes earlier. Would the snake have been in this spot? Would Lucy have noticed it before it launched an attack at them?

Lucy takes in a breath and exhales. "It's a snake. Let's move slowly to the right." Even though it has food in its mouth, Lucy doesn't want to continue on the path just in case it feels threatened, drops the food and lashes out at them.

It's a reptile, so no need to worry about D63. But Lucy doesn't want either of them bitten by a poisonous snake. It would require medical attention and end the goal for today.

Unfortunately, they need to leave the path and carefully move through the grass to avoid the reptile. This is also dangerous, as she could step close to another hidden threat; it's why they are wearing some light armor. Lucy is extra cautious where she places her feet in the grass, keeping her gun ready to fire. Zach knows the drill; step exactly where she is stepping.

Lucy is thankful when they exit the long grass, with no other encounters. They proceed slowly along the dirt ground, while Lucy's eyes dart from the tree line in the distance on the left to buildings on their right, looking for any movement. Nothing. At least from what she can see.

Eventually they reach the football field. It's not a huge structure but it does have fencing and bleachers that protect against imminent threats. The field is a mix of dirt and high patches of grass that have not been cut in seemingly forever.

They head to the metal bleachers for what was once the side of the home team. There are four sets connected horizontally, each one about twenty feet in length, providing adequate room for each family to spread out.

Lucy points to the end of the first one, "Place one cone here."

Zach stops but doesn't drop a cone. He simply stares at her.

"What?" Lucy asks.

He just stares at his mother.

"What is it?"

"You didn't say please," he says, lifting his chin and looking away. "Where are your manners mom?" he asks with a comical tone.

Lucy chuckles at his obvious mocking her. "You are so correct my dear. Pleaaaaase, place a cone there."

Zach releases a grin and drops one of the cones.

Much of Lucy's life is focused on survival and giving her son stern warnings to keep him alive, so she enjoys periodic, light-hearted humor, when warranted. She walks about eight feet and points to the ground. "Place another here...Pleaaaaase."

Zach plops a second cone. "Good manners Mom." He's clearly mocking what she has said to him countless times.

She proceeds another eight feet and points. With this spacing, they should have just enough room on the bleachers for the total of eleven families and individuals who live alone, excluding Lucy and Zach.

Zach follows along and places another one. "I got it mom."

"Great. Can I have one, please?" Lucy asks, open hand extended.

He squints his eyes and offers a sly grin. He's clearly trying to think of a funny response. "I guess you can have one," he says in comical exasperation.

"I'm so grateful for your generosity," Lucy responds with her own humor. She loves her son's wit, which she thinks is unusual for a typical eight-year-old.

While he proceeds along the bleachers and places all eleven cones, Lucy walks to a spot about twenty feet away from the midpoint of the bleachers and places her cone.

Eventually Zach joins her, and they sit down on the dirt. He eyes Lucy as she opens the backpack. Lucy removes two bags, one with nuts and one with three apples. She offers him the bag of nuts, which she knows are his favorite.

Zach's eyes light up as he accepts the luxury. "And we have time to finish the story, right? How you got home? I want to know what happened to Uncle Peter." He says with a serious look on his face.

Lucy checks her solar watch and looks around. "Okay," she

concedes. "We have a little bit of time. But when people start arriving, we need to stop. This meeting is very important."

Zach nods as he crunches some nuts between his teeth.

"Where did we end?" Lucy looks up, as if the clouds offer the answer. "Oh yeah. Grandpa had saved me; and then Uncle Peter and I went to the cabin to survive. Remember, animals didn't carry D6 back then, but they were still very dangerous. Here's what happened."

TWO

Brazil – about 15 years earlier

I woke abruptly from a nightmare. My head was raised off a pillow, gasping for breath. I laid in bed, scanning a small, dimly lit room, trying to understand where I was. Shades were drawn over two windows, blocking most of the daylight. The settings were unfamiliar.

My mind was like a rebooting computer, coming to life, trying to understand where I was. I recalled the terrible dream of my father falling into darkness that startled me to consciousness. For a fleeting moment I was relieved it was a nightmare, but a flood of memories ushered me back to reality. I remembered where I was; and it was worse. Much worse.

It had been over two weeks since my father died, saving me before falling to his death. I had been in bed virtually the entire time, while my brother had done whatever was necessary to keep us both alive in this small cabin, just a short way from the tragedy. Fortunately, it was filled with supplies. Canned food. Bottled water. Rain barrels connected outside. And valuable survival gear.

The cabin was on a location high enough so that it was not affected by the recent tidal wave. The lower land had been engulfed, flattening virtually all of the foliage. But trees on adjacent hills remained, leaving portions of the jungle going inland intact.

Countless times I replayed in my mind the terrible events. The rope bridge breaking that landed me on the ledge. The cracking ledge that led to Dad jumping down to hoist me to safety, just before he fell to his death.

What did I do differently from Dad and Peter? Why did the rope bridge snap? What did I do wrong? These questions barraged my mind.

Occasionally my thoughts attacked me. *You did this. Dad is dead because of you.*

Mourning his death was a gross understatement. It was accompanied by severe depression. Extreme self-pity. Despair. I had no motivation. Zero. No desire to move. No yearning to live. I just lied there, staring at the wall. My routine was thinking, crying, sleeping.

My stomach groaned, angry with me for not eating. I had consumed only enough to avoid starvation.

Suddenly the doorknob to the bedroom turned slowly. It was obviously Peter checking in on me. My face was away from the door, hidden from his view. I didn't want to engage. After a brief moment, the door closed quietly.

My heart broke for Peter. He had tried several times to console me, telling me it was not my fault. But negative thoughts had always swept away any inkling of hope. I couldn't move on. I was in a deep, dark pit of suffering; and climbing out felt insurmountable.

Time was not healing this deep wound. Even when I tried to think about other things in life, such as survival and my family back home, despair crept back in and easily overwhelmed all other thoughts, like a flood washing away tiny insects crawling on the ground.

It's your fault. Life will never be the same. There is no way to recover.

I closed my eyes, just as a tear escaped and trickled down my cheek.

I forced myself to reflect on good memories. Dad spending time with me playing board games. Doing puzzles. Taking me out for ice cream.

I whispered to these memories, "I miss you, Dad."

Sadness. Occasional anger. Back to misery. Utter despair. These emotions were exhausting. The recollections of my father faded, and I fell back asleep.

When I woke again, I checked my watch. Only an hour had passed. There was no routine to my day or sleeping patterns.

I placed a hand on my forehead. It was clammy and gross; but I didn't care. As I moved my body slightly, I felt sharp pain in my back and discomfort in the rest of my body from being in one position for too long. I rolled over to face the opposite wall and pulled the sheet up, over my shoulder. It was damp and smelled of sweat. I took a deep breath through my mouth to avoid the stench and exhaled slowly through my nose. I wondered whether I should make myself get out of bed and force some food into my body.

I just don't feel like it, I thought to myself.

As my eyes scanned the far end of the room, I noticed Dad's backpack. It wasn't new. I had seen it there before. But for some reason I hadn't noticed that it was bulky. I felt my eyebrows furrow.

What's inside? Survival gear? Rope? Poncho?

I couldn't recall. My curiosity grew.

Why can't I remember what is inside? The mystery was consuming.

Eventually, my desire to know its contents propelled me out of bed. I pushed the blankets away from my body and swung my legs around until my feet hit the floor. I stumbled a bit. There was no question I had been lying in bed far too long. I stretched out some of the cramps, took a couple steps to retrieve the bag and staggered back to bed.

I sat up, with a bit of energy, eager to find out what was inside. I opened the backpack and pulled out a flashlight, a pencil and two books. Nothing exciting. I didn't know what I expected. I recalled seeing these items in the raft at one point. One of the books was the Bible. No surprise; I had seen Dad reading that a lot.

But the other book was a notebook that piqued my curiosity. Deciding it was worth examining, I picked it up and opened it. It had laminated pages, similar to the Bible, obviously to protect it from weather. As I flipped the pages between my thumb, it was clearly my father's writing. Lots of notes. Suddenly a small, folded paper, not laminated, fell out from the front. I quickly opened it. It was a note from my father that literally took my breath away. My left hand held the paper, shaking a bit, while my right hand covered my mouth.

Lucy and Peter,

Currently we are floating at sea with no land in sight and you are both sleeping.

I don't know what the future holds, but if you are reading this something must have happened to me. I want you to move forward, knowing that I am in a better place.

This notebook provides notes that I had taken before our trip about evidence for God and reasons to believe Christianity is true. I hope it is helpful to you. The other book is the Bible, which is even more important. They will help you decide your eternal destiny.

Never give up!

I love you very much.
Dad

Tears poured out of my eyes. I squeezed them shut, but the liquid continued to trickle out and down my cheeks. My head dropped, heavy with emotion. It was as if I could hear my Dad speaking to me. I embraced the feelings, despite the mixture of pain with delight.

For a short time, I just sat there. Motionless. A bit numb.

I yearned for more from my father and looked back at the notebook. I picked it back up and flipped to the first page, which had the following heading: *Evidence for God & Christianity.*

I scanned the pages. Each one was a separate topic, with succinct notes and a conclusion, nothing too detailed. Examples of summary points included:

- **Beginning of the Universe**: Since the universe had a beginning, something outside the universe must have caused it and only God fits the description of this cause (timeless, spaceless, immaterial, powerful, personal).
- **Design of the Universe**: The attributes of the universe (like the force of gravity) are so extremely finely-tuned to support life, that the best explanation is a divine architect – God.
- **Morality**: Since morality is objective (independent of human preference) and applicable to all people, the source must transcend humankind – God.
- **Bible (reliable)**: We can be confident we have the author's original content since thousands of manuscripts, including early ones, enable us to cross-check if there are variants.
- **Bible (true):** We can believe the authors recorded the truth because they included embarrassing details about key figures as well as many archaeology discoveries that support the accounts.
- **Bible (divinely inspired)**: The Bible claims to be inspired by God, which is supported by numerous fulfilled prophecies as well as one central message of salvation disclosed progressively over many centuries thru about forty authors.
- **Jesus (identity)**: Jesus clearly claimed to be God based on statements He made about Himself and actions He performed (forgave sins, accepted worship, etc.); and Jesus's earliest followers made direct claims that He is God.
- **Jesus (proof)**: Jesus validated His claim to be God by living a sinless life, performing miracles and rising from the dead.

These were things we discussed just weeks ago. Argued about is more accurate. Reading them later? It was surreal. Butterflies exploded in my stomach. I even felt a hint of nausea, but I couldn't stop. It was a way to connect with my father.

I pressed on, reading the points on each page with genuine curiosity. It gave me purpose, a much-needed break from misery. But it was more than an emotional connection. I was a bit intrigued with the information.

Am I really interested? I wondered.

Even if most of my desire was for emotional connection, I did sense in myself a hint of intellectual curiosity. Surprising. Stunning.

I considered my prior mindset – apathy. Before my father's death, much of my life was an *I could care less about what was true about God or life after death.* I was focused on the here-and-now. I didn't want to waste time on something no one knows the answer to. Life is too short. When I turned sixteen, I channeled my anger at God, annoyed my parents put so much emphasis on this belief system I thought was insane.

But now it seemed there was nothing more important than the truth about God. Because, ironically, life is short.

If there is a God, is my father alive? Does he have a soul that is now in heaven?

My father's death was like a wake-up-call. Other aspects of life that seemed important at the time were so trivial when compared to our fragile mortality.

Apathy toward God? Indifference about spiritual truth? I now realized this was short-sighted and foolishness, considering what is at stake. Eternity.

Is this really me, thinking this way? I wondered.

I was a bit awestruck with myself. This was a massive change of direction – a 180-degree reversal, so to speak. Before today, the only time I took an interest in God was to channel my anger or antagonize my father.

For the next few hours, I made my way through the entire notebook, soaking in what was clearly my father's words. There was some new content I had never heard before. Insight related to logic, the soul, archaeology, Jesus's resurrection and more.

The resounding theme throughout the notebook was that the Christian worldview about God, sin and salvation is ultimately what is true about the universe, humanity and heaven. My mind was dizzy from the information. Even though my Dad shared a lot of it with me, my perspective was completely different.

Clearly, I started reading these pages simply to hear his voice through the words he wrote. But somewhere along the way, I started consuming the information without immediately dismissing it as foolishness.

Was I now simply hoping it is true? Had my mindset changed a bit because part of me desired it to be true for my father's sake? Was I falling prey to wishful thinking? Misplaced hope? Blind faith? Was I considering the possibility of God because it was now my preference?

No. I was a skeptic by nature. I couldn't change that. But a barrier seemed to have crumbled, and I was now considering the information with an open mind.

Open mind. Was I not open-minded before? Probably not. Dad said we all have some pre-conceived notions of reality that can make it difficult to be truly open to insight that may alter our opinion. I thought I was so smart.

If I was brutally honest now, the rationale for God and Christianity seemed to make sense. A lot of sense. Something had clicked, like suddenly solving a math problem. At a minimum, it seemed more likely than not that it is the truth. Wow – that was what Dad said countless times.

One of the last pages included a point from my father stating that evidence for God should not take precedence over reading the Bible.

I glanced at the waterproof Bible and picked it up. For such a long time I spurned this book. I constantly rejected it. No way would I be weak enough to embrace what it said, was my mentality.

Apathy and closed-mindedness – enemies of seeking truth. My father's words echoed in my mind. I nodded, as if agreeing to read the Bible with an open mind, something I really had never done before.

I felt the dryness of my tongue and parchedness of my mouth. I was beyond thirsty. Tears had not helped matters. I grabbed a half-filled bottle of water and chugged the rest. I felt the sensation of fluid hitting my empty stomach.

I should eat something. Later, I decided. I propped up some pillows, sat back and opened to the Gospel of John, my Dad's favorite.

After a couple hours of reading, I heard the front door to the cabin open and slam shut. Obviously, Peter had returned to the cabin from wherever he had been. I hoped it was Peter. Otherwise, I had an intruder. I listened intently and recognized the shuffling footsteps were his.

I continued reading the Bible. It drew me in, to a point where I didn't even feel the hunger pains that I knew must be there. I read for the rest of the day and into the night, using the flashlight. I didn't need rest. I had overslept for days. I was captivated by the life and ministry of Jesus. I was surprised at how different it seemed with an open mind. I believed. I believed it is the truth.

Periodically my eyes filled with tears, considering the love Jesus had for humankind. His compassion for people. His great sacrifice on the cross as a way of salvation for those who will accept it.

I was flabbergasted that reading the Bible seemed so different. Prior to now, if I read it all, it was done as a chore. But now I was reading it with an open mind and a genuine desire to learn about Jesus. To understand who He is and what that meant to me. I felt my heart stirring, a feeling that was growing with intensity.

At some point in the middle of the night, I was completely overwhelmed with emotion. I put the Bible down, got out of bed and knelt with my face on the floor.

I prayed to God.

> *I'm so sorry. I have been selfish. I know I'm a sinner. I treated my Dad terribly as well as others. Please, please forgive me. I believe in you God. I really believe in You. I believe in you Jesus, that you are Lord. I believe you died for me. I believe you rose from the dead. Please forgive me. I accept you as my Lord and Savior.*

My body quivered as I poured out my testimony to God. But after a short-time I felt relief. I felt lighter, as if a tremendous weight of guilt had been lifted from my shoulders. I was astonished by this sudden transformation. Never did I think I could change my outlook so quickly.

I looked up, as if peering through the ceiling of the cabin, all the way to heaven. *Thank you. Thank you God.*

I climbed back into bed and resumed my reading position. I was too emotional for sleep. I had joy. Joy! The pains of sorrow were gone. Guilt about my Dad's death was no longer attacking me. Despair was no more. The change in my emotion in such a short time was astonishing.

I felt…reborn. I wanted to survive. I wanted to find a way to get home.

THREE

My eyelids slowly cracked open. Through narrow slits, I noticed a few lines of light at the window, the sun shining around the drawn shade. Daylight. I had fallen asleep, and the Bible now rested on my stomach. I noticed my mouth was parched and tongue felt like sandpaper. I was clearly dehydrated.

I heard Peter milling about on the other side of the wall. Nothing too noisy. Then an opening and closing of the front door.

I checked my watch. 9:12 am. I had slept several hours. Must have finally conked out, after many hours of reading. I rubbed my eyes and stretched my legs, attempting to shake off the drowsiness.

Yesterday seemed like a dream. A good dream. Seeing my Dad's notes. Reading about God. Evidence for Jesus. I had not forced it. Things clicked – made sense, really. I still had that wonderful feeling of hope. A fresh beginning that had rejuvenated my spirit.

I tossed the bed covers aside and sprang out of bed. Opening the door, I peeked into the main cabin area and found it empty. Obviously. Peter was outside. Who else would be here?

I entered the main portion of the cabin and immediately grabbed a bottle of water to quench my thirst. With the rain barrels attached to the cabin, water was plentiful. I then took a large bucket of water and headed back to the bedroom. I gave myself a quick sponge bath before putting on fresh clothes. I pulled my hair back and used an elastic to tie a ponytail. It felt good to be moving with a purpose.

I returned to the main portion of the cabin to satisfy my hunger. Food was getting scarce. There was a good supply when we arrived, but we had been burning through it quickly. I devoured a granola bar to get something in my stomach. I closed my eyes to enjoy the flavor. The honey and raisins were delicious. Then a second bar, this time chocolate chip. The sugar exploded in my mouth. I realized I hadn't tasted food the past couple weeks, rather I was simply consuming calories to survive.

As I finished my last bites, I took notice of the cabin. It was certainly not as tidy as I preferred. Some empty wrappers and open cans on the floor. Granola bars scattered about. Buckets of water in different spots, as if carried in from outside and randomly dropped. While certainly not a survival priority, it gnawed at me. I felt a bit anxious about it. I'm a perfectionist; my brother's a slob. But who was I to judge? I had done nothing to help Peter.

With my hunger and thirst satisfied, I decided to spend a few minutes making the place more orderly, appeasing my angst. I threw away trash and put some order to our food and water sources.

As I was organizing, I noticed a large, folded paper on the main table of the cabin. It was obviously something Peter had taken an interest in, as I know it wasn't there previously. I unfolded the thick paper, which opened to roughly two feet on all sides. A map.

I sat down to examine it. Initially, I didn't understand the array of circles and lines; and I didn't comprehend the words that were all in a foreign language. Then it became obvious one side of the map was water and the other was a large landmass with a pointy section. I could see now that it was a topographical map that displayed elevation. The pointy section was a cliff. A rectangle with an "X" on this hill must be the cabin that was sheltering us. It's difficult to know how much area the map covered, but it seemed to be maybe fifty miles based on a scale at the bottom. Then I noticed a circle drawn lightly in pencil around a structure, at what seemed to be about twenty-five miles away. The structure was on the water but connected to the land with what looked like boats. A marina, I guessed.

Did Peter circle that? Is he thinking that's our way home?

Peter. He didn't know I was up and about. I decided to go find him.

As I exited the cabin, the sunlight blinded me. I shielded my eyes with my right hand and took in a view of the ocean. It was a peaceful day. The sounds of waves below the cliff were faint, but noticeable. Other than one massive tree to my left that was close to the edge, it was open space – left, right and ahead. On either side there was a steep drop to the bottom. I didn't dare look farther ahead, a quarter mile away where the tragedy occurred.

Since my father fell to his death, I had not gone near any edges; but for some reason I felt an immediate need to overcome this emotional obstacle. To eliminate this psychological barrier.

I walked over to the large tree to the left and placed my hand on it. I leaned forward and peaked over the edge. It was a good fifty feet to the bottom, where large, jagged rocks protruded from the sand.

My knees began to quiver, nervous from the height. The recent events flooded my mind, tormenting me, shattering my peace. I began to feel light-headed. My body started to tremble, and I quickly backed away, afraid I might faint and fall over the edge. I felt my body sweating, far more than what the warm air warranted. Suddenly I vomited the granola bars eaten just minutes ago.

Bent over, with my hand on my knees, I could only shake my head in frustration. *Well, that was not a success.*

I took a deep breath to calm my nerves. I closed my eyes and inhaled the salty air again, pausing a moment to gain my composure.

Then I recalled my initial reason for coming outside – to find my brother. *Peter must be behind the cabin somewhere.*

As I circled around to the back, expecting to search for my brother, I found him sitting on a small rock in open space, about thirty feet from the back of the cabin, facing the jungle. There were only a few trees in this large open area, before the start of the jungle that was about one hundred feet beyond Peter. The dense jungle Peter was facing survived the tidal wave only because it was at a higher elevation, but to the left and right, where it dropped off, much of the foliage was either knocked down or washed away.

I made my way toward him through the wavy grass, When I was about half-way, I hollered, "Peter!"

He visibly jumped a few inches off the rock, clearly startled, as if I blew a whistle to wake him from sleep. I fought the urge to break out in laughter. I wasn't trying to surprise him, but it was amusing, nonetheless.

His face showed an expression of shock. He grabbed his heart. "You scared me!" Then the sides of his mouth turned upward, revealing a smile.

As I arrived within a few feet, his eyebrowed furrowed, as if confused. "You're outside. I mean…it's good. But…are you smiling?" he asked me, as if he had never seen that expression on my face.

I realized that I was, in fact, smiling; I was happy to see my brother. He was holding a heavy rope in his hands that extended about seventy-five feet toward the jungle, to the biggest tree that was still in the open space. The long rope hung over a large branch, tied to small piece of metal mesh and what looked like netting spread over the metal.

"What are you doing?" I asked, ignoring his previous question.

Peter turned back to the tree, "Trying to trap a bird."

I looked around the sky and didn't see anything flying about.

"They're around," he said, also looking up. "Frigatebird, I think they're called." He pointed toward the tree. "I put some granola on the ground, hoping one will land, so I can trap it."

I considered asking whether he had the gumption to kill a trapped animal, and the knowledge to clean and cook it; but I refrained, thinking it's unlikely he'll catch one.

I leaned down and gave my brother a hug around the shoulders. "I'm so sorry I haven't been there for you." I felt him shake a bit with emotion.

He rubbed his eyes and sniffled, as if fighting back his feelings. "I thought I was on my own," he confessed, his voice breaking up a bit. This pained my heart. I'm his big sister; and while our relationship includes pestering each other, I've always felt a responsibility to take care of him.

"No more," I responded, sitting down on the ground, to his left.

His head was down, as if embarrassed by his emotions. It felt good to be with my brother.

Sensing awkward silence, and wanting to avoid getting emotional myself, I decided to change the subject. "Is that the direction of the marina?" I asked, pointing across his face, to the right.

Peter lifted his head and looked in that direction, "Yeah." He turned back to me with a confused expression, "How'd you know?"

"I saw the map."

"Hmmm. Yeah. I don't know." Peter muttered. "Maybe there's a boat to get home." He shrugged his shoulders in a pessimistic gesture. "Not that either of us know how to drive a boat."

It was a fair point. Neither of us knew how to operate any kind of watercraft. Who knew if there was even a boat there? But what else were we going to do? Live here? Try to survive on a ravaged coastline?

Peter pointed to the jungle ahead. "We would need to go through there, and around." His head and finger followed to the right. "Find some way back down to the coast and follow it to the marina, I guess."

I examined the dense jungle ahead, again, noticing that most of the low points of the coast had been ravaged by the tsunami a few weeks ago; but there were a series of hills that still had trees and thick foliage. The thought of entering the jungle brought back the recent memories of danger we encountered. Snakes. Spiders. Alligators.

"We'll need to move carefully, but we can do it," I stated with optimism, choosing to fight my fear with determination.

"Wow. What's gotten into you?" Peter's facial expression had changed back to bewilderment. "Don't get me wrong. I'm mean, I'm glad. But...you're depressed beyond words for over two weeks and now you're...good to go?"

"I found Dad's notebook about Christian apologetics. I read it for a while and then the Bible." I gathered some internal confidence to make my declaration. "I've decided to put my faith...my trust in Jesus. I'm a Christian."

Peter chuckled, slapping his knee with his left hand. "Yeah. Okay sis." He tapped his chest, "I tell the jokes, remember?"

He stared at me for a moment and then his expression slowly

changed from amused to confused. "You're serious?" his eyebrows furrowed. He looked stunned, as if I just revealed something that was beyond shocking. Like I was a secret agent from another country, masquerading as his sister.

Was it so hard to believe I had changed my beliefs? I was a bit annoyed. Not sure what I expected. Maybe some happiness for me. Nonetheless, I maintained my composure, choosing not to scold my younger brother.

"Yeah. Dad's notebook had all this evidence for God and Christianity. You know, the stuff he shared with us, and even more. It was...amazing. At first, I just wanted to hear Dad's voice, but I also liked the evidence for God. Then I started to read the Bible with an open mind, and it just spoke to my heart." My hands circled around each other, gesturing that everything happened quickly. I carried on about my reading, but I could tell I was starting to babble, so I got to the conclusion. "I just decided to be a Christian."

"I...I don't know what to say," Peter shook his head back-and-forth. "Just like that. You changed...Why?"

"It's the truth." I answered sharply, as if it should be obvious to him.

He chuckled again, and extended his left hand, palm upward, toward me. "Wait. This coming from the person who used to say, 'All truth is relative. We all get to decide our own truth.' What happened to that?" His eyes were begging for some kind of reasonable explanation.

"Well...that was wrong," I responded, shrugging my shoulders.

Peter frowned, as if underwhelmed with my response. "So... truth is not based on personal opinion or perspective?"

I recognized he was quoting my previous mantra, something I used to say a lot to counter my parents; that I have my own truth that works for me. It sounded great at the time, but now I understood that that idea was definitely wrong.

"There are some things that are true based on our opinion," I conceded. "Like my favorite music or what I think is the best book. Dad says that is called subjective truth, because it truly is based on the opinion of a person, the subject. But the idea that all truth is subjective, based on someone's opinion, is simply false; it's called relativism[3], and it's not possible. There are countless things that are true, independent of our opinion, like the car is blue. That's called objective truth, because the truth is based on the object, not anyone's opinion."

Wow. I surprised myself that I was able to remember Dad's notes.

"And here's the key point bro," I said, hands in the air for emphasis. "The truth about God and life-after-death is not based on personal opinion. We don't get to pick what we prefer. We don't decide spiritual truth. We discover it!"

I noticed Peter's jaw ajar. Stunned. "Who are you? What have you done with my sister?" His eyes narrowed, as he looked at me suspiciously, and smirked. "Are you an imposter? An alien that has taken over her body?"

I punched his arm playfully.

He turned back to the trap, dangling in the air. There was quiet for a moment, until he interrupted the silence. He chuckled. "I'm living in an alternate universe," he said, shaking his head.

I looked ahead at the jungle, scanning for wildlife. A few birds in the trees, squawking loudly. "I don't believe in aliens or alternative universes," I said in a friendly, matter-of-fact manner.

More silence went by before Peter interjected with a question. "So, truth is not whatever feels good? Or whatever we prefer?" he asked in a mystified tone, again quoting what I always used to state as a fact.

"Dad wrote that truth is what corresponds to reality.[4] It's not based on what makes us feel good, or what we prefer." I nodded my head as I spoke. "I know. I know. That's opposite from what I used to say, but Dad was right. It's not possible for people to have different perspectives that contradict and both be true.[5] That's logically impossible."

"Wow!" Peter's expression was shock. Then he looked at me with astonishment. "Wow. That sounds like Dad."

I felt a warm, satisfying feeling throughout my body, as if

someone just gave me a great compliment. "Well. Dad was right," I said, matter-of-factly.

"Well okay then. Whatever works for ya." He turned back to look at the jungle.

The last comment annoyed me. It flew in the face of what I just said. *It's not what works for me.* I thought to myself. *It's the truth. Did he listen to what I said?* But I decided not to push it. I didn't feel like arguing. I was happy to be with my brother. I followed his gaze, looking back to the jungle. "We need to take plenty of supplies to make sure we get to the marina."

"Mmmhhhmmm," he muttered in agreement.

Our conversation was suddenly interrupted by a huge bird descending close to the tree ahead, flapping its large wings as it landed near the food. We both went silent, not wanting to scare the bird away, even though we were seventy-five feet from the fowl.

It was just out of reach of the trap and seemed to be inspecting the food. I felt myself holding my breath in anticipation. After another moment, it hopped forward and stabbed toward the food with its beak.

Peter released the rope, and the contraption crashed to the ground, capturing the animal. It flapped feverishly. The trapped animal bounced around a bit, but Peter's invention seemed heavy enough to detain the bird.

We simultaneously jumped to our feet and began to run to our successful capture. But we stopped suddenly when a massive jaguar jumped out of the jungle and sprinted toward the imprisoned bird.

I froze in terror, my eyes wide with shock. After a few strides, the jaguar was within range and pounced on the defenseless bird. I saw the beast bite at the bird through the contraption.

Without speaking a word, Peter and I both began to backpedal. Slowly.

The huge jaguar ripped the bird free from the contraption. It engulfed the hapless fowl in its mouth, taking large bites, crushing the victim in its mouth. As it chewed its food, its head turned to our direction. It seemed to be eyeing us as it finished chomping and swallowing its prey in mere seconds.

As we continued to creep backward, I saw the jaguar begin to take a couple steps toward us. Instinctively, I turned and sprinted, "Run Peter!" I screamed. "Run!"

I felt a jolt of terror run through my body. I pumped my arms and legs as fast as possible, trying to make sure I didn't stumble. If I fell, I knew I was dead. The cabin was twenty feet away. We raced frantically.

Peter was slightly ahead of me. If someone was going to get caught, it was me. I had a sense that at any moment, the jaguar was going to pounce on me, just as it had just done to the defenseless bird. Claws in my back. Teeth at my neck. I didn't dare look back to see how much the jaguar had closed the gap, even though it was terrifying.

Peter made it to the corner of the house and turned to head toward the front door. Just as I was turning the corner, the jaguar's claw caught a piece of my shirt toward my lower back. The jaguar's claw ripped a piece of fabric away from me as it tumbled several feet ahead. I raced to the front door, which Peter held open for me, screaming for me to hurry.

I jumped inside, rolled several feet and turned to see the beast had gotten to its feet and started to sprint toward us. Peter slammed the door and bolted the lock, his body braced against the door for support. I raced to the door and pressed my shoulder against it.

A second later, I felt a tremendous crash against the door. It shook my body, literally rattling my jaw. If we were not pushing against the door, I believe the hinges would have snapped and door collapsed to the floor.

I heard scratching on the other side of the door, claws scraping wood which offered only a few inches of protection from the beast. I wondered if the door would hold the enormous jaguar if it charged again.

"Peter! Get a chair!"

He grabbed a chair, and we propped it under the door handle, angled as a brace. I pushed on the legs, wedging it into the wooden floor to lock it in place. Without a word, we both grabbed the wooden table and pushed it against the door, over the handle, for more support.

We both stopped and listened. Several moments passed without any sound from outside. All I could hear was our heavy breathing. I looked around the cabin. Noticing the windows, I wondered if the jaguar could launch itself through them.

"Peter. Duck down. Just in case it sees us through the windows."

We both crouched down behind the table. Waiting. Listening.

"We're trapped," Peter whispered. "How are we going to get out of here?"

"I don't know," I answered between breaths.

Gradually, our heavy breathing diminished. Then it occurred to me. That thing might be very hungry because the tsunami washed away most of the ecosystem. But the jaguar wasn't the only one facing a limited food supply.

My mind started racing. *At some point, we are going to run out of nourishment. Staying here isn't a long-term option. But how can we traverse the jungle with that beast outside? Is there a realistic way to make it to the marina?*

For the first time in my life, I considered prayer to be a suitable response to a crisis.

FOUR

I had never been more nervous in my life. I took deep breaths to calm myself, but it didn't help. I felt myself trembling.

I watched Peter finish eating his second granola bar; and I felt I should also consume calories. Energy would be important for the physical task we were about to attempt, but there was absolutely no way. Last time I ate and approached the edge of the cliff, I vomited every morsel from my stomach.

After being chased by the jaguar, Peter and I spent the last four days contemplating what to do. Our situation was dire. We were trapped in the cabin with a food supply that was almost gone, while the jaguar wandered around outside, waiting for us to emerge, like a cat prepared to pounce on the mouse that exposes itself.

Peter didn't recall seeing the jaguar the first couple of weeks, but now it seemed to be lingering in the area. One time we exited the cabin to see if the jaguar had left and saw it sitting on the roof. We slammed the door just in time. Another time we spotted it walking in front of the trees at the edge of the jungle, about a hundred thirty feet away. To avoid the predator, Peter came up with a plan that I considered insane.

At first, I was adamant I was not going to do it. My fear of heights and the painful memory of Dad falling to his death made the idea unthinkable. While Peter wasn't thrilled about it either, he finally convinced me that we really had no other choice. After two days of debate, and tearful memories, I consented to the plan. The alternatives were starving in the cabin or taking a chance in the jungle with the massive cat roaming about; neither was a viable option.

I wrote a note to the owner of the cabin, thanking whoever they were for the shelter that allowed us to survive. I thought about leaving our address so they could ask us to reimburse them for the food and survival items we were taking, but it seemed like a silly idea given the state of the world.

The idea of taking these items gnawed at me. *Are we stealing?*

But since no one had been here in almost a month and the world was facing an apocalypse, we reasoned it was okay for our survival. I hoped someone would not come to the cabin hoping to find items and not have them. It was too late regarding the food, and we only took the survival items we felt we needed for a three-day journey. At least we hoped it was only a short trip to the marina.

Peter and I shouldered our backpacks. Then we each grabbed opposite ends of a coiled rope. It was thick, good for climbing; and we estimated it to be about one hundred fifty feet long, more than enough.

I took one last look around the cabin that had provided shelter for us the past three weeks. I felt nostalgia. To me, it was more than just a refuge; it was the place where I had made a decision to change my life. My eternity.

I locked eyes with Peter. Neither of us said a word. We both knew we were about to risk our lives. Either this bold plan would work, and we would escape; or, one or both of us would be badly hurt...or worse. I tried to convince Peter to accept Jesus as his Savior in case he died, but he said he was already a Christian. Was he? I didn't know, but I resisted my desire to push him. I wanted to, but Dad said you can't force someone to accept the truth about God, and trying to do so can backfire. I relented, trusting Dad was right.

We both scanned the outdoors through the windows. We hadn't seen the jaguar since yesterday afternoon. It was now mid-morning. *Where is it?* It would be better to know, but we couldn't wait. I couldn't wait. I barely slept last night, tormented by the task ahead. We nodded at each other without a word. It was time for action.

Peter opened the door and we each stepped out, just a short way. He scanned the left and I surveyed the right, checking the surroundings for danger, ready to jump back inside to safety. But there was no sign of the beast.

Actually, it was a nice day. Warm temperatures and no precipitation right now, which was especially important. We both exited the house entirely, checking the roof, listening for a hint of movement. Nothing.

Peter crept over to the left side of the house and peered around the corner.

"See anything?" I asked softly.

"No," he whispered back, continuing to look around. "But it could be in the back of the cabin."

It could be anywhere. Edge of the jungle. A mile away. Or resting close by in a place we couldn't see.

"Once we start, we're committed," Peter said, looking back at me. "No turning back." We had already discussed that, but I guess he felt the need to remind me, one more time.

I swallowed the collection of saliva that had accumulated in my mouth from nerves. I inhaled a breath through my nose. *Don't think about it*, I told myself. I exhaled slowly through my mouth. "Let's go," I said, along with a sheepish thumbs up.

Peter looked in my eyes and mouthed the words, "One...Two."

"Three," we said together.

We both ran alongside each other, carrying the hefty rope and heavy backpacks filled with supplies. In less than ten seconds we reached the large tree. Peter circled around it once, with the rope in hand. As I waited, I couldn't help but look over the edge. The view sent chills through my body. Nausea hit me hard. *That was a mistake!*

I started to feel my body go numb, paralyzed with fear. *No,* I told myself. *Don't think. Keep moving!*

I dropped the rope next to me and pulled the backpack off my shoulders. I found the bushes below that Peter had mentioned and tossed my backpack toward them, hoping for a soft landing. I watched as it flailed about in the air before crashing successfully into the foliage.

"Lucy!" Peter yelled.

I jumped, startled by his scream. I saw him pointing at the jungle. My nerves exploded when I saw the large jaguar sprinting toward us.

Peter threw his backpack over, and then we simultaneously grabbed our respective ends of the rope and tossed them over the edge. We both laid on our stomachs, grabbed the rope and swung our feet over the edge. No need to speak. We had discussed the plan many times yesterday.

As I committed to hanging over the side of the cliff, I saw the jaguar closing fast. *Don't think! Keep moving!* I descended a few feet, but a flood of terror hit me as I realized I was fully over the edge, dangling fifty feet in the air. I gripped the rope tightly with hands and feet.

"Climb down Lucy!" Peter yelled.

"I can't," I cried. The fear of heights. The trauma of Dad. "I can't!"

The appearance of the jaguar directly above shocked me. It growled in anger, showing its large teeth. The scare gave me a jolt of adrenaline and I started to climb down, just as it reached down with its claw and took a swipe. Fortunately, I was just out of reach. My eyes connected with the eyes of the beast. It snarled at me, seemingly frustrated at not being able to reach its meal.

"Hurry!" Peter ordered. "We need to climb down together."

As I gripped the rope, I felt sweat on my hands. I was afraid I might slip, or my strength would give out. But my desperation to survive enabled me to hang on. It was terrifying to alternate releasing each hand to climb down, but I made sure to cup my feet tightly around the rope. *Don't think! Keep moving!*

Without a word, we both continued to climb down, staying about the same level as we descended. It was hard work. I felt my muscles burning, straining to hold my weight. But I was determined not to fall. The lower we got, the better I felt.

Within a few minutes we arrived at the bottom of the cliff.

"We made it!" Peter declared, slapping my back as I tried to catch my breath. "I knew it!"

I didn't say a word. I was trying to collect myself. I looked back up to the height from which we started. Tears filled my eyes, as I grasped what we had just accomplished, avoiding the dangerous jaguar and the peril of falling.

"Are you okay?" Peter asked.

"Yeah," I muttered, closing my eyes, relieved it was done.

Just when I thought I was coping, a deluge of emotions released inside. The dread of heights. The trauma of my Dad's death. After hours of panic, it was finally over. I was on the brink of sobbing. But I refused.

I won't cry. It's time to be strong, I told myself. I bit my bottom lip to fight back the emotion and opened my eyes. *It's time to move forward. It's time to be strong!*

As Peter walked over to retrieve the backpacks in the bushes, I took in the surroundings. The coastline was a disaster. At this lower elevation, the tidal wave knocked down trees and left a maze of foliage.

I scanned from right to left until I came to the cliff we descended. I pondered for a moment until a thought resonated. While it was a long way up and around to the cabin, I realized the jaguar wasn't a long distance away. We needed to flee this area.

When Peter returned, I reached out my hand to take the backpack. "Let's get going," I said. There was nothing breakable, so there was no need to check. "We only have so much daylight."

We began to hike along the coast, which was no easy task. We continuously climbed over small trees and navigated around large obstacles. The sun was hot and the hiking laborious. The heat baked rotting fish left from the tidal wave, giving off an awful stench. I noticed a few birds and rodents eating the dead sea creatures, but there wasn't any dangerous wildlife to fear. I was surprised there weren't more scavengers consuming the fish; but obviously they were washed away with the massive tsunami.

After a couple hours of walking, we were finally past the natural disaster, back in the jungle. We tried to stay on the coast, but there were times when we encountered an obstruction, and it was easier to travel through the jungle. The familiar shrieks of the rainforest, chirping birds and howling monkeys, were daunting. We stayed within sight of the water to follow the coastline.

With our bodies tiring, our pace slowed to plodding. We decided we needed to stop for a break. Finding a clear area amongst the trees, with rocks to sit on, we lowered our backpacks and settled down for a rest.

I removed the canteen from my backpack and took a large gulp of water, swooshing it around my mouth. I wiped the matted hair on my sweaty forehead to the side. My body was drained.

"Two days of hiking is gonna be tough," Peter stated, as he took a bite of a granola bar.

I swallowed a second swig of water. "We might make it sooner. I'm more worried about finding it. If we somehow miss it by going inland, who knows where we end up." I couldn't bring myself to eat another granola bar right now. It's all I had eaten the previous few days. I was more thirsty than hungry anyway.

Peter finished eating and grabbed a long stick, which seemed good to assist with hiking. "Do you want one?" he asked.

"Nah," I shook my head. "Thanks."

After twenty minutes, we resumed our trek. The jungle was dense. The air was thick with humidity, making breathing more difficult.

We stopped again after two hours for lunch. More granola bars – sheesh. And then hiked for another four hours. We were exhausted, physically and mentally. Then I saw big trouble ahead.

"Stop!" I ordered Peter.

We both froze.

"What?" he asked. "What is it?"

"Up ahead." I pointed. "The marsh up ahead. See the alligator."

A giant black caiman monster was close to the path we were headed.

I looked around. The ocean was to our right, over a hill, but this portion of the jungle we were standing in had few trees and quite a bit of marsh. I noticed an alligator to our left, about a stone's throw away. The terrain ahead looked the same, as far as I could see. I spun around and noticed the landscape behind us was the same. We had been walking in this type of environment for some time without my really thinking about it. Then I noticed the sun was descending behind the trees to our left.

I started to panic, which must have been noticeable to my brother.

"What's the matter?" Peter asked. "Let's just go around."

"Where? This marsh is all over the place and the sun is starting to go down. It's going to be dark soon. We should have stopped a long time ago."

But I was too tired to notice. Too drained to focus on anything but putting one step in front of the other.

Peter's expression turned to concern. He pointed to a large alligator thirty feet behind us, slowly crossing the path we had just traveled. "We're surrounded. What do we do?"

I looked around, searching for an idea. I felt the remaining sunlight ticking away, increasing my anxiety.

"Can we build a fire?" I asked.

"How? This place is so wet and there are few trees," Peter answered. "I say we run for it."

"Are you insane?" I snapped. "We could run right into an open jaw. And who knows how far the marsh goes," I said pointing ahead where there was no visible end to the marshy environment. "Even if we make it a short way, it'll be dark. We won't be able to protect ourselves."

"Well...what do we do?" his voice was tense. I was trying to stay calm, but I was stressed as well.

As I scanned the trees closest to us, I got an idea. I removed my backpack and unzipped the top, continuing to watch my surroundings for danger. "Take out your hammock," I told Peter, as I removed mine.

He looked at the trees. "Oh yeah," he said, indicating he understood my idea.

We had taken two old rope hammocks from the cabin thinking they might be useful to keep us off the ground, away from creepie crawlies on the jungle floor. But now I hoped they would protect us from larger predators.

Fortunately, some trees close by were at a suitable distance apart to hang the hammocks.

"How high should we tie them?" Peter asked.

"I don't know. As high as possible."

We were able to climb a short-ways and tie them about eight feet off the ground. Within minutes the sun began to dip below tree level. As darkness quickly descended on us, we took refuge in our hammocks. One end for both hammocks was tied to one tree, with each of the other ends tied to different trees, keeping our hammocks close together.

As the light faded, the sounds of the jungle intensified. Birds squawked loudly. Insects chirped. Leaves rustled from movement. The eerie sounds were popping up all around us. I had forgotten what it felt like to be in the open jungle at night. Danger lurking everywhere.

I tried to ignore it, but the wildlife racket was maddening. Peter and I had few words to say; and after twenty minutes, I decided I needed a distraction to settle my nerves. Something to take my mind off the raucous noise around me.

I took Dad's notebook out of my backpack, along with a small flashlight, and settled into my hammock.

"Are you gonna read?" Peter asked, shocked at the idea.

"Why? Is the light gonna keep you awake?" I asked sarcastically. I wondered if it was too snide, but it had been a while since I had teased my brother.

"Yes," he responded with a jab of his own. "As a matter of fact, I think it will interrupt my beauty sleep..."

"And you need all you can get," I interrupted. "Too easy."

It's one thing we had always done; light-hearted verbal jabbing each other. He's better at it, which sometimes annoyed me.

"Seriously though. How can you read right now?" Peter asked.

Jason M. Jolin

"It gets my mind off things. Reading Dad's notebook helps."

"Helps with what?"

"When I read his words, I feel like I hear his voice. It's a lot of things he told us, but...new stuff too."

"Like what?"

"Really Peter?" I asked suspiciously. "I thought you didn't care about evidence for God."

"You like it because it's from Dad...maybe I will."

"Okay. This page is about logic."

"Forget it. I'm out." Peter chuckled at his joke. "Kidding. I'm kidding. Please sis...read me some logic stuff."

Either he's going to annoy me or fall asleep. I thought. *Probably the latter.*

"Dad wrote, 'Logic is rules for the right way to reason.[6] The correct way to determine what is true. And God is the best explanation for why logic exists'."

"I never heard Dad say this. Are you messing with me?" Peter asked dryly.

"I guess it's not a common argument for God, but I think it's interesting. People use logic all the time."

"Really? I never use..." Peter paused, and quickly pivoted. "I mean I do use logic all the time."

"We all do. Here's an example from Dad. If someone said, 'Everyone in the house is sick, Bob is in the house, therefore...'"

"Bob is sick," Peter finished. "See I'm smot! I keep telling you that sis."

"The conclusion follows based on the rules of logic. If instead, we said, 'Therefore, it's raining outside.' We would all say that doesn't work. There are rules for the right way to reason."

"I knew I didn't like philosophy." Peter yawned.

"Okay. Are we done? Can I read to myself now?"

"I'm kidding," Peter pleaded. "Please, this is good stuff," he said with a bit of sarcasm." Why is God the best explanation for logic?"

I rolled my eyes, irritated at the need to continue, but I acquiesced.

38

"Okay. Here's how Dad summarized it. Is logic material or immaterial?"

"What?" Peter asked.

"Dad wrote that question. 'Is logic material or immaterial? Can you touch or see these rules?'"

"Umm...obviously logic is not material," Peter said in a tone that the answer was obvious.

"Right. Second question. Is logic objective or subjective? Subjective means that people are the source of logic, and we can simply change the rules to reason however we want. Objective means the rules exist separate from our opinion, meaning people don't create the rules for logic."

"I suppose it's objective," Peter answered. "Not sure where this is all going. Sounds like a bunch of stuff that makes my head hurt."

"It's actually pretty interesting. Just follow the summary. Logic is kinda like math. The rules are immaterial. They're also objective, meaning they exist separate from people's opinions. Given that, doesn't it make sense that logic came from an intelligent source outside of humankind? In other words, God?"

"Whoa. This is way too deep." Peter laughed.

"I don't think it's that difficult. There are immaterial rules for correct reasoning that apply to all humankind. They cannot come from matter. They need an intelligent source, a mind that is beyond people. In other words, God."

"Okay," Peter sounded uninterested.

Our conversation faded, but I continued to read for a bit.

After some time, I decided to try to get some sleep. I turned off the flashlight and closed my eyes. The noises barraged my sanity. Fortunately, I was very tired. I started to cup my hands over my ears, when I heard a scuffle directly below me. Some kind of animal shrieked in agony and then went silent.

"What was that?" Peter asked anxiously.

I turned my flashlight back on and looked over my shoulder toward the ground. A large caiman alligator sat on the ground almost directly below me.

"Oh my goodness. Alligator," I whispered. "Peter don't make any sudden movements. Don't want our hammocks coming loose."

"Thank goodness we're high," Peter whispered back.

I let out a large exhale and turned out the light. "Let's just try not to move or make any sound."

"Yeah…Okay."

After a few minutes, I heard what sounded like movement below, followed by hissing. Loud hissing, like that which would come from an angry alligator. I tried to ignore it and settle my nerves, but the thought of hanging in an old hammock with alligators underneath me was terrifying. My imagination about the dangerous reptiles walking around in the dark just below us increased my anxiety. A visual of four large alligators, powerful jaws open, waiting for me to fall, entered my mind. There was no way to rest.

After several more minutes, I heard scratching on the tree that my hammock was tied to, the part that was closest to my feet. The trunk of the tree shook slightly even though it was fairly large.

"What's that?" Peter asked nervously.

I clicked the light and examined the tree.

"It's climbing!" I screamed. *Alligators can climb?!*

"What?" Peter yelled. "I don't see it!"

I felt sheer terror. I pulled my feet close to my body, away from the tree. I quickly reached into my backpack tied to the tree next to my head. I ripped open the top zipper and felt inside for the gun I'd taken from the cabin. I pulled out the six-round revolver that had three bullets. Peter had wanted to take it, but I somehow convinced him it was safer with me, the older sibling. I hoped I would never use it, fearful about the possibility of having to aim at a person, but now was glad I had the weapon.

"Peter. Grab the flare gun in your backpack."

I aimed the flashlight at the tree and saw the alligator had climbed up several feet, about halfway. Another wave of terror filled my body. I aimed the gun at the large beast. It was hard to pull the trigger, so I dropped the light in my hammock and used both hands to squeeze the trigger. I could no longer see the alligator, but I aimed in the direction I remembered.

Bang!

The blast was deafening. After a moment to gather myself, I flashed the light on the tree and saw the alligator was no longer there. I searched up, down and around the tree, making sure it hadn't just moved to a new area, not that it was likely for the beast to scamper around the tree.

"Did you hit it?" Peter asked.

"I think so. Fire the flare at the ground."

I heard Peter snap the trigger. The flare hit the dirt below and lit up the area with a bright red light. I saw a couple alligators scamper behind patches of long grass, which were scattered around. Hissing continued from multiple directions in the darkness.

I shined the flashlight on the other trees around us, checking to make sure no other cold-blooded predators were approaching. All seemed clear, for now.

"What do we do?" Peter asked.

"I don't know...I don't know."

The sounds of the jungle came alive. Either they had paused from the gunshot, or I had subconsciously blocked them out when the action unfolded. The screeching insects echoed in the darkness, bombarding my sanity.

Peter clicked his flashlight on and searched all around with me. But after a couple minutes of searching, we couldn't find any alligators. The flare seemed to have dispersed the giant reptiles.

The red light from the flare faded and the area below our hammocks went dark.

"They'll come back. What do we do?" Peter whispered.

I shined the light above my head. "Should we climb higher in the trees?" I asked. "How high can these things climb?"

We both scanned the trees with our flashlights. They were not that large and there wasn't a lot of room to go higher. In fact, we wondered if there was a chance the small branches above could break from climbing, sending us to the ground. But we couldn't think of other options. We decided it was our backup plan. Our only backup plan.

"We just need to stay awake," I said.

"No problem with that," Peter replied.

I listened intently for movement below, but the shrieking insects made it difficult.

"What if we throw food a short way away?" Peter offered another idea.

"Then what do we eat?" I countered.

"I'm not saying we throw all of it."

"I have two more bullets in the gun. Let's just keep watch for now and see if they return."

For the next hour neither one of us slept a wink. But eventually exhaustion started to overtake our concern, as no other sign of danger emerged. We decided to take turns keeping watch, allowing each of us to get a few hours of sleep. One of us, at all times, continued checking the ground and trees. Only once more did an alligator approach a tree near us and begin to climb, causing a stir. But without any action from us, it seemed to lose interest and walk away.

We were so thankful when light began to peak over the horizon. It's not as though the sun's radiance would cause the alligators to clear out, but at least now we could see potential danger. Everything seems scarier in the dark. It had been a terrible night. My nerves were shredded from hours of worrying.

When the morning sun fully illuminated the area, we climbed down from the trees with our backpacks. We couldn't untie the hammocks because the knots were extremely tight, and we didn't want to stay in the area more than a couple minutes. Peter cut them down with a knife so we could take them with us.

For the next hour, we carefully traversed the marshy area. It is as if we were walking through a minefield. We stayed clear of patches of long grass that could be hiding a caiman alligator. We saw a few of them, but none were close to us. Eventually, we cleared the dangerous area and hiked for another hour; then stopped for a break and some breakfast. I couldn't help but lay my head down and fall asleep.

CHAPTER
FIVE

During early afternoon, the skies opened up, releasing a torrential downpour. The rain was good for drinking. We opened our mouths to catch the much-needed water; and filled the canteens we had brought with us. But getting drenched was very uncomfortable. Our shirts and shorts were heavy. Our soggy sneakers squished with each step.

The large drops of water pelting the leaves throughout the jungle was loud. The sounds of chirping birds had gone silent. Perhaps they were hunkered down, waiting for the storm to pass. Or maybe the sound of rain showering the trees was drowning out their chatter. At one point, we heard a crackling of thunder in the distance.

The shower was relatively short, but it left us soaked. The weight made progress even more difficult. We were also exhausted. The lack of sleep had left us with little energy. Despite these struggles, we forced ourselves to press on.

We were aware that our exhaustion could cause us to become careless, so we reminded each other to be careful where we stepped, identifying areas that demanded extra vigilance. Long grass that could be hiding a poisonous snake. A low hanging branch that could be concealing a deadly spider. When possible, we stayed in open areas, away from foliage, and watched for signs of large predators.

"I'm not sure I can keep going," Peter said, as he leaned against a tree and rested his head on it. He was breathing heavy. His eyes revealed his fatigue. I was also tired but wanted to make a little more progress. We still had a few hours before we needed to think about sheltering.

I looked around for a place to rest, but nothing looked safe. Clusters of trees, large leaves and thick bushes, "I don't see a good spot to sit. Can you go a little further?"

"I'll try," was all Peter could muster.

I started to become concerned about my brother. "You need to drink water. You might be getting dehydrated. Do you feel okay?"

"I'm just tired," Peter said as he reached for his canteen.

I reached over and felt his forehead for a fever, wondering if he could be sick. Normally Peter would have pushed my hand away, but he didn't seem to have the desire. "Your head is a little warm, I guess. But I think it's just from hiking. It's not like your burning up."

We decided to push on for a short time, but our pace was quite slow.

When we found an open location, we rested for a good thirty minutes. Peter actually dozed off for a short time while I kept watch. I sat in my drenched clothes, worrying we could be getting lost, praying that God would help us. I hated the sogginess of my shirt, hanging heavily on my body. It was so uncomfortable. There were more important things to worry about, but it nagged me. And I knew it would be with me for some time. While the air was warm, it was very humid.

"Do you feel better?" I asked, when Peter's eyes fluttered open.

"A little," he said as he sat upright. After taking a minute to gather himself, he was ready to resume. "I can walk for a little bit."

I watched Peter get up to make sure he really could handle walking. He seemed better. "Okay. You go in front of me."

We trudged through the jungle for another hour. Peter was sluggish. It was obvious he was drained. Apparently, lack of sleep was hitting him hard, so I was thankful to spot a place I thought would be a good shelter.

"Hey. Look," I said, pointing up a small hill to a cave.

"You really want to go near a cave?" Peter asked. "Remember the last one? Spiders? Bats?" The tone of his voice revealed his concern.

"We won't go too far inside. Maybe we can start a fire. Scare away critters. Dry our clothes."

Peter thought for a moment. "Alright. I'm beat. But if we can't get a fire started, we need to build a shelter away from the cave. And I'm not going too far inside."

"Deal. Do you want me to carry you up the hill?" I joked.

Peter rolled his eyes at me, and then we started to ascend the hill. "Actually, yeah. Can you carry me now?" He responded with his own sarcasm.

As we approached the cave, we could tell it was shallow, and no apparent danger. The mouth of the cave was not narrow; it was about twelve feet wide, making it more of a large concave in the side of a hill. We dropped our backpacks at the entrance and removed our flashlights. We shined the light inside confirming in was only about ten feet deep and no open crevices.

Maybe that's good, I thought. *Nothing hiding deep in a cave, jumping on us from behind.*

"Why don't you gather firewood while I clear out the cave a little and make a campfire?" I suggested.

"Sure."

"You must be tired. You're not arguing at all."

Peter didn't answer. He started to gather branches for firewood. I grabbed a stick and used it to clear away leaves that had apparently blown into the cave. Unlike moist leaves on jungle ground, these leaves were dry and crispy, great for a fire. I noticed spider webs in a few corners that I wiped away but didn't see any eight-legged terrors.

Not finding any suitable rocks to build a campfire, I dug out a small hole at the mouth of the cave, just under the overhang in case it started to rain. I then assisted Peter in collecting firewood; most of it was damp, but some seemed fairly dry.

As Peter took a break, I gathered a bunch of dry leaves, rolled them together like a small stick and placed it in the makeshift firepit. I placed several small twigs on the rolled-up leaves and then some dry branches.

I wondered whether Dad would be proud of my first attempt. I quickly dismissed the thought to avoid getting emotional. It was hard enough staying resolute, trying to survive. I couldn't let myself think about my father who died less than a month ago.

I removed waterproof matches from a small cylinder and struck a match against a rock. It didn't catch. I tried again and failed. I grabbed a new match, and it ignited right away, surprising me. I lit the leaves and a few twigs. The flames built quickly.

"Wow. I'm impressed." Peter stated. "So would Dad."

I felt the emotions flooding back in, breaking through the doors I had barricaded shut, overtaking my composure. Before I could hold them off, a couple tears leaked out. I looked away, gathering a couple sticks while I wiped my eyes.

"I'm sorry," Peter said. "I didn't mean to…" his words tailed off, apparently not knowing what else to say.

"It's okay. Really." I emptied my mind and ignored my emotions. It was the only way to suppress my sorrow. While I no longer felt guilt, I was still mourning for my father. We both were. I placed a couple larger sticks on the fire. "How are you feeling?"

"Better than before." Peter sat inside the cave to the right side, close to the fire, with his legs extended and feet crossed. He pulled out a sealed package of trail mix we had taken from the cabin and started to consume scoops of nuts, raisins and dark chocolate.

After placing some wet branches around the fire to dry, I did likewise, sitting to the left side of the fire. I needed a break and something to eat. I crunched on the trail mix, relishing the salty flavor. The food hitting my stomach felt so good. We had not eaten much during the day. I washed it down with several gulps of water. We had plenty of rainwater to stay hydrated.

When I finished, I took a long, sturdy stick I had found and carved a point with the four-inch knife we had taken. It took twenty minutes, but I was pleased with the spear. It was strong and sharp.

I looked over at Peter whose eyes were closed. He was clearly beat. We both sat for a while. Drying by the fire. Resting.

The sunlight was beginning to fade. A veil of darkness was

descending on the jungle; and with that, the nighttime insects began to chirp.

I started to feel antsy. My body was tired, but my mind was restless. I needed to do something. I pulled out Dad's notebook and with a flashlight started to skim some sections I had already read. I had always been one to review important information, knowing that the key to learning and remembering things is repetition.

"You're reading again?" Peter asked, startling me.

"I thought you were sleeping."

"Just resting."

"One of us should get sleep while the other keeps watch," I suggested. "Do you want to go first?"

"Sure," Peter agreed. "Maybe you can start talking about philosophy again. That'll put me to sleep."

"Oh yeah? When you fall asleep, I'm gonna find a giant spider and put it on your neck."

"That's really not funny," Peter snapped back.

"Maybe I wasn't joking," I countered, even though I was. "Maybe I plan to get even with you for all the times you annoyed me by finding big spiders to put down your shirt and small ones to climb in your ears."

"Lucy!" he yelled.

I cracked up in laughter. "I'm kidding! Really. I'm kidding. Sorry, that was too far."

"Okay. Ha. Ha. Now I can't sleep. You go first," Peter said in an animated fashion.

"No. I'm going to read. It relaxes me."

"Dad's notebook?" Peter asked.

"Yup."

"What does it say?"

"It doesn't say anything. You actually have to read the words." I teased.

"You can read?" Peter returned with his own joke. "Wow, when did you learn?"

"That's the brother I know," I said, with a big smile. "I was getting a little worried about you today."

"I was getting worried about me too," Peter said. "Again, what are you reading?"

"This part is about Jesus. Reasons we can believe He is God, as He claimed to be; therefore, we can trust what He says about spiritual truth. I'm starting to review the evidence for His resurrection. Remember the acronym Dad taught us?"

"Yeah...uh...ACE...Right? Am I right?"

"Yeah, but do you remember what ACE stands for?"

"Ants...Crawling...Everywhere." Peter chuckled at his bad joke.

I rolled my eyes. "Your hopeless."

Peter's face turned serious. "Hey, maybe I'm making an observation. We are sitting on the ground."

Peter smirked, not able to keep a straight face; but the thought of ants and other insects crawling around began to gnaw at me. I was keenly aware of the possibility when I first sat down, but being reminded of it made me increasingly anxious. We had cut the ropes on our hammocks and couldn't think of a way to hang them to hold our weight. I moved even closer to the fire, so the heat was slightly uncomfortable.

Peter laughed and then abruptly stopped. Something must have triggered in his mind, probably spiders, because he then slid closer to the fire as well.

I broke out in laughter in a manner I hadn't done in months. The irony of him making me uneasy had boomeranged back to him. Apparently, Peter didn't like my response, as he quickly reverted to the original topic.

"I remember. Give me a second," Peter said, looking up, as if searching for the answer. "Appearances...Conversions...Empty tomb."

"Wow," I was genuinely impressed. "I really didn't think you remembered." I didn't think he cared about the topic or paid attention when Dad talked.

"I tell you all the time. I'm smot."

"I agree bro. You're smarter than I give you credit for."

"Wait. Did you just give me a compliment?" he asked playfully. "You truly are an imposter. I knew it. Someone has taken over your mind."

"Ha. Funny," I said with a smile. "I'm trying to be a little nicer." I resumed reading, reviewing the current section.

After a few seconds, Peter inquired, "What's next? Ask me another question."

I could tell his curiosity was piqued. I didn't know whether it was interest in the topic or wanting to hear the written words of our father. Maybe both.

"So right now I'm reading the reasons these three points are considered historical facts. What are the reasons to believe Jesus really appeared to His disciples? Why believe that Paul and James really did convert from nonbelief to belief? Why believe Jesus's tomb really was empty?"

I looked at Peter, "How would you defend those facts?"

"I would say...I'm starting to feel drowsy."

"Good. I'll wake you in a few hours," I knew he was joking.

"I'm kidding. I want to know. I kinda like hearing Dad's words too."

I was a bit torn. In one way, I wanted to just read to myself. Soak in Dad's words and let the positive feelings resonate in my soul. Wait. Did I just admit I have a soul? Yeah. I mean, that is the Christian belief. I just never actually admitted it in my mind as true.

While I wanted to read to myself, it felt wrong to exclude him; and my selfishness gnawed at me. Besides, a small part of me was glad Peter was interested. I told myself it would be interesting to quiz him.

"Let's start with this. Why believe Jesus appeared to His disciples after the crucifixion? Why believe they had real experiences of the risen Jesus?"

"Ummmm...The Bible says so...I have no idea," he conceded.

"Actually, that's partly right. Dad states that these events were written in multiple, early sources."

"Multiple sources?" Peter asked. "You mean beyond the Bible?"

"Technically, the Bible is sixty-six books combined into one book. So, actually it includes multiple sources. The appearances are recorded in the Gospels of Matthew, Mark, Luke and John.[7] It's also cited by the Apostle Paul when he quoted an early Christian creed that listed appearances by the risen Jesus[8]. This important creed is dated very early, probably within two to eight years after the resurrection.[9]"

"Okay. Okay. It's written in multiple sources."

"No that's a big deal. Multiple, early sources are important to historians when validating ancient events. It's a good reason to believe these documented appearances are not a legend that developed over time."

"Okay. But aren't they a little biased? They could have been lying," Peter countered. His tone was serious. Not sarcastic. He sounded a bit like me, thinking critically; and I was playing the role of Dad. It was kind of bizarre, but I liked it.

"Dad is one step ahead of you," I said "He has two main reasons why we can believe this written testimony. Number one, the Bible includes some embarrassing details in certain events. If the authors were making all this up, they would have portrayed the disciples in better a light."

"Give me an example," Peter demanded.

Where is the sarcasm, I wondered. *Where are his jokes?*

"Okay. Dad's favorite is Matthew 28:17, where it mentions the eleven disciples with the risen Jesus, worshiping Him. But it also says that some doubted. While it's understandable people could be skeptical someone coming back life, it is an embarrassing admission that some of Jesus's disciples doubted. It indicates the author told the truth, because if they were making up a lie, they would not have included the detail that some doubted."

"Wow. Dad is debating us even when he's gone." Peter chuckled.

I paused at the comment, not sure how I felt about it. But then decided to continue. "Another reason to believe they told the truth regarding appearances is they were willing to suffer, and even die for these claims.[10] Some people are willing to die for a belief, but the disciples were different. They were in position to know whether their belief was true or false, and they would not have been willing to die for a lie.[11]"

"You got all that?" I asked. "There's gonna be a test."

"Is it open book?" Peter smiled.

"Nope. You need to remember everything," I rebuked him in a fun way and flipped the page. "Next is 'C', which stands for Conversion. Why believe Paul and James really converted from nonbelievers?"

Peter snored loudly, in a manner obviously faking sleep.

"I knew my dim brother couldn't stay awake," I said aloud.

"I'm wide awake. But I have no idea," he confessed.

"Paul's conversion is recorded in the Bible. His attack on the Christian church before his conversion is included in one of his own letters[12] as well as Luke's account in the book of Acts.[13] And then Paul has an encounter with Jesus that leads to his conversion which is recorded in Acts.[14] Why believe this actually occurred? Paul suffered for his claims as a Christian, which is recorded in the Bible[15] as well as early church fathers, such as Polycarp[16] and Clement of Rome.[17] Clement of Rome and Tertullian wrote that Paul died for his faith.[18] That a former enemy of the Christian church converted to Christianity is amazing!" I said in a loud, exhilarating voice.

"This is interesting stuff," Peter admitted. "But not sure I'm going to remember half of it. I'm not taking the quiz."

"You don't have to remember all of it. But it's interesting to know there are good reasons to believe in the resurrection. Switching to James, the half-brother of Jesus, the Gospels record that Jesus's brothers did not believe His claims to be God when He was alive.[19]"

I looked up from the notebook. "That's not hard to believe. If you claimed to be God, I'd think you're insane. Then again, you might be anyways."

Peter smiled. I decided not to ask what was running through his imagination. I resumed reading.

"What would have changed James's mind from being a skeptic of his brother to believing He was resurrected? Probably only an appearance by the risen Jesus, which is recorded in the early creed I mentioned.[20] Later, Paul meets with James in Jerusalem when he is a believer.[21] We can believe James's conversion because he is willing to die for this claim. The Jewish historian Josephus, not a Christian by the way, records that James was stoned to death for his belief.[22] He must have been truly convinced."

"I'm still stuck on your insult," Peter said. "If I claimed to be God, you wouldn't believe me sis? I mean, I am extraordinary."

I ignored his quip.

"Finally, the empty tomb. It's recorded in all four Gospels.[23]"

"Yes, but why believe these claims in the Bible?" Peter challenged. "I'm not easily convinced you know."

That was a clear mockery of me. "Hey, are you imitating me? You don't have the brain power." *Was that too snarky*, I wondered. That's odd; I never worried before about being too snide to my brother. That is more than once now that I've said something I immediately worried was rude.

Peter countered my question, "Nah. I would need to be more fiery and irritable," he jabbed.

Irritable? I know it was a verbal jab, but it stung a little. I don't want to be known as irritable. After a few seconds, I asked. "You got an answer? Why believe Jesus's tomb was empty? Are you thinking? Wait. I see smoke. Is that just the fire in front of us or is your brain overheating?"

"Just staring at movement in the jungle. It's a lot scarier at night."

I scanned the area. Darkness had overtaken the jungle. Noises sprang out from different locations. But what was truly eerie was periodic movement, swaying branches and rustling leaves. My mind started to imagine potential threats moving about; but I decided to ignore them rather than torture my sanity with unknown predators lurking around us.

"Umm," Peter interrupted my focus. "I don't know."

"JET," I answered.

"What? I don't hear a jet."

"No. JET is an acronym for the reasons to believe the tomb was found empty.[24]"

"Oh. Too bad. I thought you heard a jet." Peter chuckled at his joke.

"'J' stands for Jerusalem factor, meaning that both Jesus's crucifixion and resurrection appearances occurred in Jerusalem. It would have been impossible for this belief that Jesus rose from the dead if His body was still in the tomb. Therefore, the tomb must have been empty."

"Got it," Peter gave a thumbs up.

"'E' stands for enemy attestation. Jewish leaders who did not believe in Jesus claimed that the disciples stole the body. This reaction from certain Jews is recorded in the Bible[25] and in the 2nd century by Justin Martyr.[26] The fact that enemies of Christians said His disciples stole the body, strongly implies the tomb was empty."

"Did you hear that?" Peter asked.

"Hear what?" I asked. "There are lots of noises. You aren't used to it by now?" There was scattered movement in the jungle and the darkness made it eerie, but I guess I liked letting myself be distracted with Dad's notes.

"Yeah. Okay. Enemy attestation...I got it," Peter's words tailed off as if he was distracted by something else.

"T stands for testimony of women." I continued, not knowing if Peter was paying attention. "During this first-century, the testimony of Jewish women was considered inferior to a man.[27] Given that, why would all four Gospels record the women being the ones to find the empty tomb?[28] If the authors were inventing this story about the empty tomb, certainly they would have had the men discover the empty tomb to ensure credibility for their claim. But since it's the women who find the tomb, this implies that this truly was the case that they discovered the empty tomb. Those are basically Dad's words that I paraphrased."

Peter didn't say a word. I could tell he was studying his surroundings.

"And there you have it," I concluded. "Some very good reasons to believe the three historical facts about Jesus's resurrection. Appearances. Conversions. Empty tomb. And these are historical facts that the large majority of scholars who study this topic agree with, even those who are not Christian.[29]"

Peter let out a loud snore. It was clearly exaggerated, signaling he wasn't sleepy.

"Okay numbskull. You already did that joke. Don't ask if you don't want me to talk anymore."

"Just kidding sis. I really did like it. Really. It felt like listening to Dad."

"You need to try to sleep. At some point, I'm going to want to."

"Sure. I'll snap my fingers and get four hours," Peter said sarcastically.

"Good. Start now." I mirrored his sarcasm.

Our banter faded. Other than the sounds of the jungle, the fire crackled loudly. I added some wood that was previously damp, hoping it had dried enough. It was a good-sized fire that also kept away annoying insects.

I scanned the jungle, looking for danger. My eyes were heavy, causing me to fight my fatigue. I wonder if I should ask Peter to let me sleep first. I'll give it twenty minutes and see if he is sleeping.

Suddenly I noticed some bushes moving about twenty feet away. My eyes narrowed, straining to focus. At first, I didn't see anything unusual. But then I noticed two small lights.

Eyes! I thought. *Are those eyes?* I remember my father saying he saw two eyes that ended up being a jaguar. *Am I imagining this?*

"Peter," I whispered. "Peter!" I called a little louder.

"Hmm?" Peter moaned. "I thought you wanted me to sleep."

"I think I see eyes."

Peter quickly sat up.

I pointed toward the bushes with my left index finger, while my right hand fumbled around the dark, searching for my spear.

"I see it," Peter said. "Is it eyes?"

Suddenly a large animal jumped out of the bushes, racing toward the cave. It was on Peter in seconds, grabbing his right foot with its jaw, and what I'm sure were sharp teeth.

Peter screamed in pain. "Ahhhhhh!"

Light from the fire revealed it was a large jaguar. Was it *the* jaguar? The one that had stalked us at the cabin? Had it tracked us to this location? Whether it was or not didn't matter. It was attacking Peter. The powerful beast began backpedaling, dragging its victim, my brother, toward the jungle.

My hand found the spear and I instinctively started running toward them. I wasn't thinking; I was just going into action. Fear of losing my brother was stronger than my fear of the beast.

Peter flailed about, screaming in anguish.

I caught up to them just as the jaguar was about to enter the thick jungle. I stabbed at the jaguar with the sharp end of the stick. The spear seemed to penetrate its neck rather deeply. It was an odd sensation, as if I had found a soft spot to puncture. The wounded animal released Peter and flailed about. The jaguar's convulsions yanked the spear from my hands, but it remained inside the injured animal. It growled as it attacked the stick with its paw.

I grabbed Peter and began dragging him away from the beast. He shrieked in pain, but I didn't stop. I knew Peter was hurting but I needed to get him away from immediate danger. I continued until we were back at the entrance of the cave, close to the fire.

I was panting, gasping for breath. My heart was racing. Adrenaline coursing through my veins. I needed another weapon. I used the small bit of light from the fire to locate my knife. I grabbed it and turned back to the action in a ready position, worried the jaguar may be charging at us. But I watched as the jaguar continued to struggle. The spear seemed to fall out, but the animal's movements slowed; and then, it collapsed.

"Peter!" I called to my brother who was now motionless. "Peter!" I shook him. He was unresponsive. I looked at his left foot. There were open wounds from the bite marks, but not too bad. Unfortunately, it was angled in an unusual direction, to the outside, almost perpendicular. Clearly broken and grotesque.

Jason M. Jolin

I wanted to vomit but resisted. I ran to my backpack, snapped it open and yanked items out, haphazardly. I found the medical kit and snapped it open, sending supplies flying through the air. I found a small bottle hydrogen peroxide and also grabbed a cloth from my things.

I ran back to Peter, hoping he was just unconscious. I opened the bottle and poured its contents on what appeared to be open wounds. I started to wrap the cloth around the wounds of his foot. As I tied it tight, Peter snapped back to consciousness.

"Ahhhhh!" he screamed, reaching for his leg.

"It's okay!" I hugged my brother tightly, careful not to touch his foot. "It's okay."

He stopped screaming, but his body trembled violently. I wondered if he was going into shock.

I continued to hold him tight to reassure him, not really knowing how bad he was injured.

Peter's body seemed to settle. "What happened?" he muttered.

"You don't remember?"

"Something attacked me. But it's a blur."

"It was a jaguar," I answered. "I think it's dead."

"You think?" he muttered weakly.

"It's dead," I said with more certainty. I inhaled through my nose and released a large exhale through my mouth. I whispered, "It's dead."

CHAPTER
SIX

I woke to the sound of chirping birds and morning light penetrating my eyelids. I had been awake most of the night, petrified the jaguar was somehow still alive. Scared another dangerous animal was eyeing us in the darkness, waiting for the right moment to strike. The slightest sound of movement wreaked havoc with my nerves. Wicked images of predators formed in my mind as I studied the dark scenery. My eyes strained to rationalize my surroundings. Light from our small fire didn't travel far enough, and barely kept us warm during the cool night.

Peter's sounds of agony during the night were gut-wrenching. He was silent for long periods of time, but then suddenly yelped. I assumed it was from sharp pain; but maybe he also had nightmares. Other times he wept softly, clearly in anguish. I hugged him tight as if that would soothe his suffering. I don't think it helped; but I didn't know what else to do. His whimpering tormented me.

Eventually last night my adrenaline subsided, and my body succumbed to exhaustion. I just couldn't stay awake the whole night even though it left us vulnerable. Our only protection was the fire, which was now smoldering.

My guess is I slept a couple hours. These nights of limited sleep were mounting. I could feel the puffiness of my eyes and overall fatigue in my body. My leg muscles ached from overexertion.

I just wanted to rest, but the fire had dwindled too much. It was on the verge of going out. I needed to take care of Peter. Keep the fire up. Get some food. Form a plan.

I pushed myself to a sitting position and scratched my face to shake off the slumber. I got to my feet and checked my surroundings. First the jaguar. There it was, lying on the ground, head facing us, eyes closed. It was a beast. Even the motionless corpse was frightening.

The chatter of birds was constant. The sounds of night had yielded to the morning shift, which was far less intimidating. Was it simply a matter of being able to see during the day? No. The sounds of night were more frightening. I was convinced.

I considered checking Peter's foot, but decided I couldn't handle looking at it yet. He was sleeping, stable for the time being. That was enough.

I grabbed some dry leaves from inside the cave and sprinkled them on the fire, followed by small twigs. I gently blew on the embers. It worked. The leaves ignited. Small flames lit the twigs. I added kindling and decided to let that catch.

We needed more wood, especially since I had no idea how long we would be here with Peter's mangled foot. There was a small supply from what we previously gathered, but I needed to get more wood to begin the drying process.

I decided the first priority was retrieving my weapon. I slowly approached the jaguar to get my spear. I crept quietly, as if it may be possible to wake the savage animal. I kept studying it, looking for any hint of movement. But the body was motionless. There was no rising and receding of the torso from breathing. The hole in its neck was gaping. *It's dead*, I kept telling myself.

My spear was lying next to the carcass. The top of the weapon was stained red. It was dry but the color contrasted sharply from the rest of the wood. My heartbeat increased as I approached. My eyes were fixed on the jaguar as I closed the distance. Its mouth was partly ajar, showing a large fang. The massive paws rested on the ground, hiding its sharp claws. As I stopped at the location of the spear, a few feet from the jaguar, I felt myself trembling. Slowly, I knelt by the spear, picked it up and quietly backed away. I felt so much safer having a weapon to defend against danger.

Next, I spent time gathering firewood. Stacking kindling and fuel was the priority, including branches I thought would dry out without too much trouble.

Most of my time searching was uneventful. Until I came across the biggest spider I have ever seen in my life. It was on the ground, legs sprawled out twelve inches, with some kind of prey attached to its fangs. Looked like a mouse. I was fairly confident it was a Goliath bird-eating tarantula, but I wasn't going to get close enough for an inspection. Peter would have panicked if he saw this thing. I was glad it was eating something else, but just seeing it, knowing these things were with us in the jungle, was disturbing.

I forced myself to stay busy with tasks in another area, eventually getting enough wood to last a while.

My stomach grumbled during my work. I needed some food. We both needed nourishment. Fortunately, we had a plenty of water. But we barely brought enough food to make our trek. This delay was going to drain our supply.

"Lucy," Peter moaned. I turned to see his eyes cracked open. The grimace on his face revealed his pain. I looked at his foot. In the daylight the angle of his foot was even more revolting; even with part of it hidden by the cloth tied around his ankle, I could see the foot clearly angled out in an abnormal position. It was beyond disturbing. The mere sight made me nauseous.

"I'm thirsty," he muttered. I gave him a bottle of water, happy to do something besides stare at his injury.

"How bad is my foot?"

"Awful," I said without any consideration to being sensitive.

Peter placed his hand on his forehead. "What are we going to do?" His voice cracked as he started to weep.

I didn't know what to say. We were facing a massive problem. Peter said the pain was bearable when he didn't move it, but any motion or touching was excruciating. The last month of events and being on our own to survive had caused us both to mature beyond our age. But the current adversity was too much.

God? Please help us. I pleaded in my mind.

I hadn't thought to pray. I had always depended on myself. This

Christian faith was new to me. Could I depend on God to help us? I now believed God was real and Christianity was true. I trusted Him to save me from judgment. But would He help us now? Dad had said there's no certainty God will remove every pain and obstacle in this life, but when we commit to follow Him, He would save us from our sins and be with us during this life.

God? If it is within your will, please help us. Please give me courage. Please help me to know what to do. I beg you. In Jesus's name. Amen.

Was that right? I don't know. Dad would tell us: *Just talk to God. Fancy words aren't necessary. God knows the burdens on your heart.*

I felt I needed to be strong for Peter. "We will be alright," I said, as I sat down next to him and put my hand on his shoulder. "Are you hungry?"

Peter shook his head as he sobbed.

"We're going to be okay," I repeated, trying to reassure him. And me.

Peter rubbed his face, wiping the tears away. He tilted his head up to look at this foot, and then dropped his head back down, in an obvious manner of disgust.

"Lucy," he whimpered. "You need to go on without me."

"Stop it!" I ordered. "Don't talk like that. I'm not doing that."

"I can't walk!" Peter exclaimed, placing his hand over his eyes.

"I'm not leaving you," I said matter-of-factly. "You took care of me. I'm not leaving you. We'll find a way."

I spent the next hour talking to Peter. Encouraging him as best I could. I needed the optimism myself. I briefly examined his foot, making sure the cloth was not leaking. While the bones and structure were clearly crushed, the open wounds seemed stable. I could not look at it for too long for fear of fainting.

Eventually, Peter ate a couple granola bars, and I had one myself. It reminded me that our food supply was intended for a short trip, not an extended stay. Peter must have been thinking likewise, as he voiced his concern. We talked rationing, and then Peter made a ridiculous recommendation.

"Why don't you cut some pieces of meat off the jaguar?" he suggested.

"Sure. No problem," I responded sarcastically. At first, I thought he was kidding, but then he kept going.

"I'm serious. It's dead. It's just gonna sit there and rot. Or something may come along and feed on it. Plus, since it bit me... I wanna bite it back."

I shook my head. "No way! Have you lost your mind? I'm not going near that thing," I said as I pointed at the carcass.

"Lucy," Peter said, somewhat irritated. "We're gonna need food. And that's a pile of it right there."

I looked back over at it. I didn't want to get close to it, let alone cut out some pieces to skin and clean for cooking. But he wasn't wrong about needing food; and that fact slowly eroded my resistance. I reminded myself that it was dead. After taking a few moments to generate some courage, I took a deep breath trying to prepare myself. I grabbed the large knife and stood. I looked at Peter who was watching me intently, as if waiting to see if I had the gumption to do it.

I willed myself to take a step forward. Then again. I approached it, slowly. As the distance closed, my anxiety increased. I got within a few feet and stopped.

Where am I supposed carve out a piece of meat? Leg? Body? I have no idea.

"What are you waiting for?" Peter hollered.

"Do you want to do it?" I snapped, looking back at him. He couldn't, of course. I wanted to suck the words back in, but it was too late. "I'm sorry. I didn't mean that." I quickly turned back to focus on the jaguar. "I don't think I can do it Peter."

I kept on guard, as if any moment it's eyes would pop open, jump to its feet and attack. I had knots in my stomach.

"Just try to slice into its paw," he suggested. "Maybe that'll make it easier after you have done it once."

The right paw was the closest part to me. I slowly, gingerly stepped closer, to within eighteen inches. My body began to quiver. I felt my nerves exploding. It was torture being this close to the animal that I believe was the one that terrorized us for days back at the cabin. The beast that sprang on us last night and severely injured my brother.

Do it! I told myself. I watched its eyes, waiting for even a tiny flicker. Ready to jump back. As I leaned forward, my hands shook terribly. I couldn't steady them.

Suddenly, a branch to my right snapped, sending a jolt of terror through my mind. I leapt backward, dropping the knife, landing on my back. My arms and feet kicked at the dirt so I could scurry backwards. As I was fleeing, I realized the sound that triggered my retreat was some other animal a short distance away, not the jaguar coming alive; but I was already rattled.

Away from the pseudo-danger, I collapsed to the ground, feeling like an abject failure. *What a wimp,* I thought. *What a weakling. It's not alive.* But I could not bring myself to touch the beast, let alone eat it. Even with no life in it, it terrorized me.

Peter consoled me, which stunned me. I expected him to scold my trepidation. But I think he was too consumed by his own predicament to chastise my cowardness.

During the middle of the day, Peter asked me to push his foot back into place. He had obviously been pondering it for a while, and even picked out a stick to bite down on while the pain tore through him. But this was simply impossible. I couldn't even look at it; how was I going to grab and twist it back into place. Allowing the thought to enter my mind, literally made me dry heave disgusting bile into my mouth. I adamantly refused. I told him I would rather cut the tongue from the jaguar and eat it raw before I could do what he was asking. Eventually he gave up and slumped back into a mix of pain and depression.

I felt like a failure for a second time in the same day. But was that a fair request? I'm not a doctor. I'm not even an adult. That was too much to ask. I don't think he could do it if the roles were reversed.

Later, I was able to gather some acai berries while searching for a little more firewood. I was cautious in the dense jungle, afraid that if I got bit by a poisonous insect or reptile, then both of us would be incapacitated. I gave myself credit for having the courage to search the rainforest after my mishap with the jaguar.

As we chewed on the berries and drank more water to stay hydrated, we both saw a lizard scurry out of the woods. It stopped in the open about a foot from the fire, as if warming itself. It was green with a body about eight inches long. We both talked about other food sources earlier and questioned whether lizards were an option. Was this a sign? Was this our chance?

"Lucy," Peter whispered.

"I see it," was my response.

I slowly got to my feet, careful not to make any sudden movements. I reached over to my backpack and grabbed a spare shirt, thinking this was the best way to trap it. The chances of my stabbing the speedy lizard with my spear was remote. Throwing a cloth over it as I jumped on it seemed far more feasible. I eyed the lizard as I stretched the cloth between both hands. It hadn't moved. Perhaps the warmth was lulling it to sleep.

Without further thought, I leapt at it, cloth extended. But as I was falling to the ground, I could see the lightning quick lizard had seen me in midair and easily scampered away. I landed on the ground with a thud. I had failed, yet again.

I withdrew, back to my previous position in the cave without either of us saying a word. I felt defeated. Sure, we were alive. That felt like a miracle considering the attack last night. Yes, we had water. We even had fire – no small feat in the jungle. But food was scarce, and Peter was severely injured. How long could we simply survive out here before nature defeated us?

"Lucy?" Peter broke the silence as a hint of darkness was beginning to emerge. The sun was dipping below the horizon. "What are we going to do?

"I don't know," was all I could say. Because, frankly, that was the truth.

C H A P T E R
SEVEN

"Lucy?" Peter said, shaking my shoulder. I forced my eyes open, almost needing my fingers to pry them apart. I was physically and mentally drained. I had taken first shift so Peter could sleep. Someone needed to keep watch for predators. Jaguars were only one concern. We stayed close to the fire to ward off spiders and ants; but given our first night, we were also worried about alligators and other hungry carnivores.

I pushed myself up by my arms to see Peter pointing at the jaguar. Two large birds sat on the carcass, pecking at its body, tearing off dead tissue to eat. They were both about two feet in size with colorful heads. Their bodies were white, and the wings had black feathers. They didn't seem to care about us.

"You don't want me to capture the birds, do you?" I inquired. Half-kidding, half-worried that might be on his mind.

Peter simply stared at them. "King Vultures," he finally said. "They're scavengers. They feed on dead animals…I wonder if they think we're next."

The words stung. He thinks our situation is hopeless. He thinks we are going to die.

"No," I said, jumping to my feet with a jolt of energy. "We won't be next. We're getting out of here," I declared.

He looked at me, astonished at my assertion. Then he dropped his head. "That's easy for you to say."

"We're getting out of here. Together," I said sternly. "Last night, while the birds taunted me from the trees, I got an idea. Do you remember that there's a road that runs along the coast? I know we wanted to stay close to the water so we wouldn't miss the marina, but the road would be easier to travel on, even if it's a little longer."

"Yeah," Peter shrugged his shoulders. His expression changed to annoyance, "But I can't walk. Are you gonna carry me?"

"No. I'm getting you crutches and we're walking there together."

His expression turned from irritated to stunned. No words followed, as if he was considering the idea. Yesterday, we briefly discussed my leaving without him to try to find help, but I decided that was too dangerous. He couldn't defend himself and even if I somehow navigated the jungle to civilization, big if, would anyone really help us with a virus possibly spreading through the country? No. This was the best way. The only way, in my opinion. We weren't going to sit here for weeks or months trying to survive the jungle while his foot healed; if it healed at all, given the crooked position. We needed to leave.

Not waiting for a response, as if the matter was settled, I picked up the large knife and walked off to find ideal branches to make crutches. I had already searched the immediate surrounding area for firewood, so I would need to extend the area of exploration.

The farther I got from Peter, the more uneasy I felt, for both of us. He had the spear in case he needed to defend himself, but there were some things he would not be able to fend off, and fleeing was obviously not an option. For me, I worried I might get lost or walk into some hazard that another person with me might have noticed. That something might be stalking me from behind or above. Periodically, I would stop and whip myself around, looking for what might be preying on me. I would then brush at my back and legs in case I inadvertently walked through a web, allowing a venomous spider to attach itself to my clothing.

Eventually, I found bamboo growing near a small stream. I selected a couple pieces about five feet in length. I cut them free, confident they would serve the purpose.

I decided to fill my small canteen, but as I reached down to the water, I noticed a large spider underneath the water. It was five inches in diameter. Not huge, but big enough to startle me. Although I didn't have Peter's phobia, it was still intimidating. Were there more? Had I walked into some kind of nest? Do they have nests? My mind was running wild with absurd possibilities. I moved upstream several feet; and, seeing no arachnids in the clear water, filled the canteen. I grabbed the two pieces of bamboo and headed back.

When I arrived, Peter had a more positive mindset. Apparently, he talked himself into my idea and was ready to try to move. I gathered our remaining supplies and filled my backpack. Peter would leave his behind and focus on walking.

I helped him get upright, balancing on his left leg, careful not to let his right foot touch anything. The cloth around the wound somewhat stabilized the dangling foot, but I could see the pain on his face. He fought through it, his expression switching back and forth between anguish and determination. He grabbed the makeshift crutches and slowly took a couple steps, being extra careful not to fall or let his right foot touch anything.

When Peter nodded that he was ready, we set off directly away from the coastline, toward where I thought we would find the road. It ran parallel to the water, so we should reach it, eventually.

Our progress was slow. I tried to take routes through the rainforest that were not dense, for fear that Peter could get tripped up. I cut a few vines that I thought were particularly precarious. Occasionally Peter yelped in pain but kept moving. I offered to help, but he refused. After thirty minutes, Peter requested a break.

I helped him get settled on a fallen tree and noticed his forehead dripping with sweat. While it was hot and humid, his effusive perspiration was clearly from exerting himself. It was obviously intense work to walk and keep his foot from touching anything. I was troubled by how much work it was to go a fairly short way. At this rate, how long would it take to get to the road? To find help? To get to the marina?

As if reading my mind, Peter interrupted my thoughts, "I can't go faster Lucy."

"I know. You're doing great," I reassured him. He was doing

great. I don't think I would have the strength to hold myself upright, nor the pain tolerance to endure the ends of the bamboo digging into my armpits, with a crushed ankle and foot hanging in pain. For some reason I expected this to be easier. I was overly optimistic that our pace would be faster.

"We're never going to get there at this rate," Peter said somberly.

"It's not a race," I countered. "Slow and steady. We agreed." I was trying to be optimistic. But inwardly pessimism was harassing my spirit, and it was building.

After resting our muscles and rehydrating, we set off again. We walked for another twenty minutes or so, at half the speed as the first stint. Peter was less stable, perhaps from being tired, so I stayed behind him in case I needed to give support. He spent more time standing still, steadying himself and resting than forward progress. I resisted the urge to show my internal distress.

As we rounded a large tree, I caught sight of a massive green snake resting on a large branch, about even with our heads, only a couple feet away. I couldn't see the rest of its body, but I immediately knew it was some kind of anaconda snake. Its head was perched, aimed at Peter's, ready to strike at any second.

Instinctively, I pushed Peter forward out of the way. He crashed to the ground and shrieked in pain. I collapsed next to him and turned to see the snake's head swaying about, as if it had attacked and missed. Would it descend from the tree and engage us in battle? Was it hungry, or had it just struck at Peter for getting too close? I studied it waiting for a clue. It seemed to settle itself back on its branch.

Peter sobbed heavily in excruciating pain.

"I'm sorry Peter! I'm sorry." I grabbed his shoulders. His body trembled violently.

Dear God, please help us. Help us Jesus! Please!

Had I injured his leg further? Was it angled a different way? Had it fallen off? I couldn't look. I turned back to make sure the snake hadn't reconsidered and decided to descend the tree limb to pursue us. It was still there, eyeing us, tongue firing in and out.

Peter wept in agony. I continued to hold him tight, not knowing what to do. Maybe we should have stayed at the cave. The situation now was worse.

Eventually, Peter stopped convulsing. I forced myself to check his foot. It looked to be in same abnormal position.

The snake worried me. In due course, it would slither down the tree, looking for a meal, and I didn't want to be six feet away from the tree.

"Peter? We need to move."

"No!" he snapped. "I can't!"

"We have to. Look at the snake!"

"Please Lucy. It hurts too much."

"No. We have to go." I got to my feet, signaling this was not up for discussion. I know I wasn't the injured one, but this area was too treacherous. I grabbed one of the bamboos, keeping a watchful eye on the menacing serpent. Peter seemed to relent to my demands, as he accepted my assistance to get to standing on his left foot, occasionally letting out a painful, "Ahh!"

Fortunately, the snake hadn't moved. But Peter was shaky. He didn't seem to have much strength, and the look on his face was pure anguish.

The snake continued to eye us. We needed to move. "Put your arm around my shoulder," I ordered

"No. I might fall!" he snapped, nervously.

He took a step by himself, with the bamboo crutches. Then another. I could tell he was in extreme discomfort. He took a few more steps. I was impressed by his ability to cope with pain and desire to push forward. My anxiety from the mammoth snake gradually dissipated. Peter pressed on, and I followed his pace, scanning for the next possible danger, spear in hand.

After less than five minutes, Peter came to a stop. He was out of breath from overexerting himself physically, taxing his muscles beyond capability. His body began to quiver. Then his arms started to spasm.

"Lucy?" he cried. "I can't...hold myself."

I ran to his side and helped him collapse to the ground. His face was white. His forehead sweating heavily. His eyes closed and body shuddered. Was he going into shock? I didn't know. I never saw anyone do that.

I removed a small thin cloth from my backpack and put it on his torso. Even though it was warm outside, his trembling looked like he needed it.

This was not going well. It was only mid-day, and we hadn't traveled far. I didn't know exactly where we were or if this was a good route to try to get to the road. Peter was physically disabled; maybe his body was shutting down. I had wanted to be positive today, confident for both of us. But this was worse. Far worse. For the first time since leaving the cabin, I felt despair. That awful feeling of desperation. I had come to hate this feeling...hopelessness.

"Lucy?" Peter spoke, eyes still shut.

"I'm here," I said, grabbing his arm to reassure him.

"You need to leave me," he said weakly, with little emotion. "I can't go on. I really can't."

"No!" I said, tears pouring out of my eyes. "I won't do it!"

I noticed a tear escape one of Peter's eyes. His trembling had slowed. Was he giving up? Was his body surrendering to the pain?

I refused to stop fighting for his survival. I grabbed a canteen and lifted his head up. "Drink some water," I demanded. He acquiesced and swallowed a few gulps of liquid. I sat in desperation, praying to God to help my brother, to give me wisdom, to do a miracle. But nothing came.

We sat together. Resting. Rays of sunlight shined between the trees. Birds chattered. A few butterflies fluttered about. I had a sense of peace. I relished the moment of rest, ignoring the long-term worries, for just a few seconds.

But reality washed away my moment. Desperation returned, causing my mind to race. Go back to the cave? Build a shelter here? I debated options in my head for over ten minutes, until I heard a familiar sound. Was that what I thought it was? Yes, the engine of a vehicle. It was faint, way off in the distance, but it seemed to be getting a little louder.

Jason M. Jolin

"Peter!"

"Mmm," he grunted.

"I'll be right back," I said, shoving the spear into his hands, dropping the backpack on the ground and taking off in a sprint. I assumed it was coming from the road we were headed for. I hurdled a rock and dodged a branch. I ran around a group of trees. I was already breathing heavy, but adrenaline had kicked in. I was sprinting for my life. Our lives.

"Help!" I yelled, hoping someone could hear me. "Hellllp!" I screamed. I couldn't shout anymore. I was panting. But I continued to run with urgency, swerving around bushes and avoiding branches.

Within seconds, I broke out of the jungle, onto a dirt road. An approaching jeep slammed on its breaks, skidding several feet in the moist gravel, stopping within twelve feet of me.

I held my hands up. "Please..." I said, trying to catch my breathe. "Please we need your help. My brother...," I pointed back to where he was, only about fifty feet away. "My brother is hurt bad. My father died."

I could see two heads through the windshield, both the size of an adult. The driver side door opened. My heart skipped a beat, thankful I found someone to help. A tall male, with fair skin, thinning gray hair and glasses, stepped on the jeep's side bar and poked his head out, over the open door.

"Get out of the way!" he hollered, motioning with his hand for me to go back toward the jungle.

What? They're not going to help me? "No!" I answered. "We need help. Please!"

The man's head dropped, as if exasperated by my request. But then lifted his chin and repeated his denial. "I'm sorry. We can't help you. There is a virus spreading. We can't take any chances. Please get out of the way." Again, he motioned for me to move to the side.

"No! I'm not moving!" I responded. I was desperate. I wasn't taking 'no' for an answer.

He closed the door and slowly started to drive around me. But I jumped to the right, keeping the jeep in front of me. I was determined,

70

resolved to either get help for my brother or get run over. There was no bluffing from my perspective.

The vehicle was now eight feet from me. I could see the two people in the front of the jeep talking but couldn't hear what was being said. They were clearly adults, whispering with a sense of intensity. I noticed a third head, this one in the back. Not a child. Another adult? I couldn't be sure.

The driver door opened. The man exited the jeep and slammed the door closed. "What's your name?"

"Lucy."

"I'm Mack. How old is your brother?"

"Fourteen. His name is Peter."

"What's wrong with him?" he asked, keeping his distance.

"He can't walk. We're not sick. I promise. Please we need help."

His eyes narrowed, as if studying me to determine my trustworthiness.

"I'm not going to get close to you yet, but show me where he is," he said.

I walked toward the jungle, eyeing him to make sure he was following, which he was, trailing me by about ten feet away. I stopped at the edge of the jungle, again checking to confirm he was still coming. Mack had crossed the front of the jeep and had continued to follow me. I entered the jungle slowly, with Mack still trailing slightly behind.

I took a few more steps, when suddenly the jeep drove off. I turned and saw Mack sprinting after the jeep.

"I'm sorry!" he shouted.

I dashed after him. "Wait!" I cried.

We were both on the dirt road, chasing the jeep that had driven ahead and stopped about a hundred feet down the road beyond us.

I ran hard, but the man's longer legs were too much. I was losing ground. He was twelve feet away from me. Then fifteen. Then twenty. He was just about at the jeep. He would jump inside and drive off.

Recognizing I couldn't catch him, I stopped and collapsed to my knees. My head dropped in defeat. I wailed in agony, not for myself, but for my poor brother, who I couldn't help. I slumped to the ground, my hands and face resting on the dirt.

Then I heard shouting. Everything was hazy for a moment, like I was in a foggy dream. I lifted my head and peered through water-filled eyes. I saw a figure approaching me, while Mack hollered at him from the outside the vehicle.

"Eli, get back in the jeep! Now!" Mack yelled with ferocity.

A tall boy with fair skin and light brown hair was walking toward me. He appeared to be about my age. He got within fifteen feet and stopped. The rear passenger door was open, where he had obviously exited.

He stared at me with eyes of compassion.

Mack hollered again, "Eli! Get in the jeep now. We almost died a week ago!"

The teenage boy turned back to his father, "She needs help. How can we drive off?"

"We need to get out of here Eli." Mack's tone was less harsh, perhaps attempting to persuade instead of order. "I'm sorry son. We can't help her."

The boy shook his head and turned back to me.

"I'm Eli," he said in a calm tone, ignoring his father.

I wiped my grimy hair away from my eyes, and tears from my cheeks.

A woman exited from the passenger door. "Eli. Please, get back here. We can't help her."

Eli ignored her. "What's your name?" he asked in a caring manner; speaking to me as if it were just the two of us.

"Please," I begged him. "My brother needs help. We need help."

"We're not staying in Brazil," Eli said. "It's too dangerous."

"We're Americans," I said. "Trying to get back home."

"We are too," he nodded. "Hoping to leave by boat."

"That's where we're trying to get to," my voice staying desperate. "Please take us." I begged, getting to my feet.

Mack started to walk toward us. Eli turned, and when he saw

his father, he began to take steps toward me. *What is happening?* I wondered.

"What are you doing Eli?" Mack stated picking up the pace. "We're lucky we're not sick yet." His tone had changed to panic.

"I'm not going to let you stop me from helping her." Eli said over this shoulder. He ran right up to me. It startled me. He grabbed my hand and turned back to his father, holding it up in the air. "There. I've touched her hand. If she is sick, I am sick."

His parents stood motionless. Stunned.

He turned back and looked down at me. He was probably six feet tall, well above my height. His blue eyes gazed into mine. His warm hand still held mine. "I won't leave you." He nodded, as he said, "I promise."

Without thinking, I hugged him.

CHAPTER

EIGHT

It had been about a month since I'd been in a vehicle. It felt strange, as if I was stepping out of antiquity into modern times, surrounded by technology. I sat in the back of the jeep, in the middle, with Peter to my right, his injured foot resting inside a folded blanket, and Eli to my left.

Not a lot was said after the family standoff – Peter and I were joining them, thanks to Eli. After the matter was decided, we had all moved with urgency. Eli and Mack jogged behind me into the woods, tracing my steps to get back to Peter. My pace accelerated as unwelcome images popped into my mind; terrible creatures attacking my defenseless brother. The menacing python strangling his torso, preventing him from calling for help. Venomous spiders sitting on his cheek, sinking their fangs into his flesh. A giant black caiman alligator approaching the scene, ready to bite his legs and fight for a share of the meal. My fast jog turned into a sprint.

But when I arrived, he was okay. No anaconda, or any other danger – *thank you God.* Eli and Mack were visibly aghast by Peter's foot; but who wouldn't be disturbed? Eli's expression was a mix of shock and disgust, while Mack's face was filled with concern. But was Mack worried about Peter's health, or how this might slow down his mission? I didn't know and wasn't going to ask.

After quick introductions, we were on our way. Eli and Mack carried Peter to the jeep. I said "Thank you" multiple times; but otherwise, there was little talking. They carefully placed Peter in the vehicle, and the rest of us jumped into the jeep. We were all in a hurry to get to the marina and leave this dangerous country. At least we all had that in common.

As the doors to the Jeep all closed, I said "Thank you," again. I couldn't help showering them with appreciation. Just a short time ago, I had collapsed in desperation; but now Peter and I had help. *Thank you God!*

I reassured them we were aware of the virus and were not sick. Mack said nothing. He was either angry or focused on tasks ahead – maybe both. He snapped the transmission into drive, and we headed off. The dirt road was fairly smooth; only an occasional bump jostled us in the back, which caused Peter to release a suppressed groan. I could tell he was trying to hide the pain.

Eli opened a backpack and pulled out two bottles of water. He handed them to me and Peter, as if knowing we must be thirsty. "Are you hungry?" he asked with a genuine look of care.

For a moment, I got lost in my thoughts. Words could not express my appreciation for Eli. Unlike his father, he made me feel welcome. Valued. Not an obstacle in the way.

"Definitely," Peter answered. "Got any pizza?"

My brother. Back to his jokes. I decided it was actually a good thing. He's not himself if he's not being sarcastic.

Eli smirked, clearly amused by the humor. His eyes shifted to me.

"I could eat something," I responded. "Watcha got?" I smiled at him, curious what could be in his backpack, hoping for something other than a granola bar.

"I don't have pizza, but not too far off." Eli removed a clean cloth. He unfolded it, revealing what looked like a couple small rolls of bread.

"It's called Pao De Queijo," Eli said. "Not that I pronounced that right, but it's yummy. It's a Brazilian cheese bread."

Mack let out a huff, as if annoyed his son was sharing the bread. Was Mack planning to eat it? I didn't want to take it if I was going to make his father mad. Maybe he was sighing at something else.

Either Eli didn't hear his father or didn't care. He offered one to me and Peter. My brother grabbed it without saying thank you and took a bite. *Where are your manners?* I thought. I considered elbowing his ribs to prompt a verbal response, but he was probably starving.

I hesitated. Eli's blue eyes gazed into mine. "It's good," he said, nodding approval for me to take it. I slowly reached out and took the offer. "Thank you. Really...We're so grateful."

Before I could take a bite, Peter grunted his approval of the bread. "Mmm...It's so good."

I studied the bread in my hands. The texture was light and puffy. I took a bite, and immediately enjoyed the flavor. The cheesy taste was delicious. I decided to chew slowly, letting myself relish the food, rather than simply swallowing it for calories.

Eli's mother turned to look at me. "My name is Ruth. I'm sorry we didn't stop. Really." Her face revealed a sense of shame, matching her words. "When news of the virus broke out, the town where we lived exploded into chaos. We...we encountered threats..." her voice tailed off, as if not wanting to elaborate. "We barely survived. We hid for a while...then gathered supplies to escape. We don't have a lot, but we're happy to help you."

I wondered if Mack agreed with the generosity. *I guess Eli gets his selflessness from his mother,* I surmised inwardly.

"I'm sorry about your father," Ruth continued. "When did he get sick?"

I realized they must have assumed he died from the virus. "No. No, he had...an accident...saving me." My eyes dropped. I didn't feel the same heavy weight of guilt, but I still couldn't bring myself to discuss the details. Thankfully, Peter jumped in with a summary of what happened.

"I'm sorry for both of you," Ruth said. "We're really sorry. We... we thought he got sick."

I squeezed my eyes to hold the tears, but one escaped. I quickly brushed it away. "It's okay," I was able to mutter without my voice cracking too much.

"I'm sorry too," Eli said, placing a hand on my shoulder.

All went silent for several minutes while Peter and I ate the bread and washed it down with fresh water.

"Do you like it?" Eli asked me, his eyes eager for my answer.

"Actually...I don't," I said shaking my head, with a look of sincerity. Eli's smile quickly faded. Seeing a hint of dejection on his face, I continued, "I love it."

Eli let out a sigh of relief, and then nodded. "You got me." *Yeah, sarcasm runs in the family*, I thought to myself. Eli's slight grin turned into a smile that for me warmed the atmosphere of the jeep.

It suddenly occurred to me that I must smell. I had a sponge bath a few days ago, and periodically washed dirt from my face and limbs, but Peter and I had been hiking for many hours. Here I sat, next to this nice boy, or young man, I don't know, and his family, and this smelly girl is sitting here polluting their jeep. *I must wreak!* I squeezed my arms tight to my body, as if that would hold the odor from my armpits. I felt gross. I wanted to shrink to a level capable of hiding in the crevices of the leather seat.

Fortunately, Ruth interrupted my frets about hygiene with small talk. We shared where we lived in the U.S., and some family background. Eli was an only child. I told them that Peter and I have three older siblings. After less than an hour, the engine went silent, and the jeep gradually rolled to a stop.

Mack smacked the steering wheel, "We're out of gas."

"How much farther?" Ruth asked, straining her neck to look through the trees. "Are we close to the marina?"

Mack shook his head, "No...uh...maybe seven or eight miles." He looked at his watch and sighed heavily. "We won't make it before dark. Too much to carry with Peter and all the supplies. We stay here tonight. Finish on foot tomorrow."

Mack immediately launched into task mode. As he exited the jeep, he gave his son a task. "Eli. Gather some firewood...carefully," he said with a point of his finger. "Ruth. Can you set up the supplies at the back of the jeep?"

Mack walked to the back and opened the hatch.

As Eli opened the side door, he asked his father, "How much wood, Dad?"

"Enough for a few hours. To cook some food and keep danger away while we eat. We'll sleep in the car."

Ruth asked Mack, "What are you doing?"

Mack pulled out a rifle, "Going to find some dinner."

"We have a lot," Ruth responded.

"We have more mouths to feed now. We need to ration what we have."

As Mack departed toward the dense trees ahead, I looked at Eli, "I can help you get wood."

"Sure," he answered.

We exited the jeep and set about searching the immediate area, gathering various sizes of firewood. Tinder. Kindling. Fuel. More than half was damp and would need to be dried out, but some felt dry enough to burn. Ruth had prepared a few supplies for dinner and was now busy picking fruit; while Peter rested in the car.

After collecting a decent pile of wood, Eli dug out a small hole on the right side of the jeep, to serve as our firepit. I helped him break some small sticks, and together we built a lean-to fire structure. He took out a container and sprinkled some liquid on the wood. "Lighter fluid," he said, as if answering a question, I may be wondering about.

With the first strike of a match, it ignited, and Eli lit the campfire. The flames erupted. We quickly added some kindling to nurture the fire. After a couple minutes, we placed slightly larger pieces; and in no time, we had a good size campfire. The sun was just starting to descend below the horizon. Our surroundings still had sufficient natural light; but it was comforting to have the fire as a source of protection.

I looked up and saw Eli gazing at the top of my head. My heart sank. Was there something on my head? A dragonfly? I had seen those around. A beetle? A spider?

"What?" I asked grabbing my head.

"Nothing," Eli answered, extending his hands in a reassuring way. "I was just noticing your hair."

Oh great. I'm more focused on survival than styling my hair, buddy. "What's wrong with it?" I asked, much nicer than my inner thoughts.

"Nothing. No," he reassured. "I was just noticing how... the light from the fire was highlighting your red hair. It looks nice."

His face sank, as if afraid he said something wrong. "I mean not just your hair. Your pretty." His eyes widened and jaw fell ajar, as if wanting to say something else, but afraid to continue speaking. It was the first time I saw him flummoxed.

But it seemed to be more than just a friendly compliment. I felt warmth flood my body. Was I blushing? I hope not. A hundred thoughts peppered my mind. Do I say, 'thank you'? Do I return the compliment? He was handsome. Maybe he's just being nice. How can I be pretty? My hair is a mess. My skin grimy. My clothes dirty. I'm a disaster!

"Ha. Your senses must be dulled from dehydration," I joked. "I know I'm thirsty. Do you have more water?" I asked, wanting to change the subject. He gladly obliged, clearly trying to recover from being flustered.

Just then a single gunshot went off in the distance making me jump. Eli didn't seem fazed. "Hope Dad got something." For a second, I wondered if that was Mack's gunshot. Maybe someone else was around. But I dismissed the thought as too much of a coincidence that the booming sound came from the same direction.

Ruth came back with an arm full of mangos; and shortly thereafter, Mack returned carrying a large capybara. He cleaned it and cooked it on a steel grate that Ruth had found in their supplies. Within minutes, a cooked portion of meat was sitting on a paper plate in front of me.

Mack woke Peter and helped him hop to the fire and sit. I cut a piece and took a small bite. I expected it to taste like chicken, but it was more like pork, and fairly salty. Not my favorite, but it was food, and I wasn't going to complain.

When I finished eating the small portion of meat and a couple mangos, I noticed Mack looking at Peter's foot.

As if on que, he said to Peter, "We really should try to straighten your foot. Make sure it heals in the right direction." Peter's face went to stone, and I got a pit in my stomach.

"That's not...gonna feel good," he replied. "I asked Lucy to do that yesterday, but that was before the extreme pain I felt." His expression slowly morphed from unease to terror.

"We can wait..." Mack offered, "...but it might be worse in the long run."

I clenched my teeth, dreading what this idea entailed.

After a bit more discussion, Peter's apprehension relented, conceding this was the right thing to do. I fretted but couldn't disagree. Peter bit down on a small towel as Eli and I each held his arms.

Without warning, Mack shifted Peter's foot back to a more normal position. Peter shrieked in pain. I held his left arm tight, "It's okay! It's okay Peter!" I yelled. But his piercing screams overwhelmed my attempt to console him.

Mack quickly tied two sticks to Peter's leg as a splint, while his upper body convulsed. Eli and I struggled to restrain him. Just as Mack was finishing, Peter fainted from the excruciating pain. I felt my ears ringing, Peter's screeches echoing inside my skull.

After a moment, Mack and Eli lifted him and placed him back in the jeep. I wanted to wander off and vomit the small dinner that churned in my stomach; but I was too shaken to walk away. Fortunately, the food stayed down.

Eli returned to the fire, and sat between me and Ruth, while Mack fidgeted in the back of the jeep with some supplies. I felt a wave of drowsiness. I was physically and emotionally tired.

"I'm really sorry about your Dad," Eli offered.

Is this guy really this nice, I wondered. But I had no reason to doubt. He seemed genuine, and I trusted my instincts on reading people.

"Thank you. It hurts, but I'm...comforted to know he's in heaven."

Eli pressed his lips together and gave a small nod. I interpreted it as being polite, perhaps not wanting to say anything I may interpret as hurtful. But I got a twinge of curiosity. What did he think about heaven? What did he believe about God? I decided to fish with a harmless question, "What do you think happens when we die?"

Eli's eyes grew wide. He opened his mouth, but paused, as if unsure what to say. He seemed uncomfortable, perhaps unaware of the topic. "I guess we go to heaven…if we're a good person?"

"But are any of us truly good?" I asked, gently. "Don't we all break God's rules?"

Before Eli could answer, Mack jumped into the conversation rather harshly, "Do me a favor. Don't fill my son's head with a bunch of nonsense."

Nonsense? I felt my irritation level jump from zero to a hundred, like a sports car going from zero to sixty miles-per-hour in three seconds.

"It's not nonsense," I rebuked. "God exists. Heaven is real," I snapped back. *Don't tell me there's no heaven. My father is there.*

Mack scowled at me. "There's no proof. You don't know with certainty that God exists."

You want to battle? I thought to myself. My mind looked through Dad's notebook, mentally flipping the pages, searching for information to refute Mack. *Ah, there it is,* I said to myself as I pictured the page in my mind. *Knowledge, burden of proof, etc.*

"What do you mean by proof?" I asked. "Do you want evidence to show it's more likely true than false, like anything higher than 51% confidence?" I was seeing the words from the notebook in my mind.

"No, I said 'certainty'." Mack snapped back with air quotes.

I frowned. "You mean one hundred percent certainty?" My eyebrows were bent with frustration.

"Yeah. You can believe in a higher being all you want, but it's just hoping it's true."

"Wait," I could tell his reasoning was wrong, but my mind was racing to figure it out. "Just because I can't show it's true with certainty, that doesn't mean the only alternative is simply hoping it might be true."

"Lucy, you can believe whatever you want, but it's just wishful thinking."[30]

"No! I believe God exists and Christianity is true based on good reasons. Even though it's not certain, that doesn't mean it's just hope or a guess. There are good reasons to put my faith in Jesus, which means to trust in Him."[31] *Did I just say all that? Wow, it was the first time I was arguing fervently for God.*

"The bottom line is you don't *know* it's true," Mack's voice was elevated. His disposition seemed to turn from annoyed to anger, but I wasn't backing down.

"So…what then?" I threw my hands up. "It's better to simply disregard the topic? That's ridiculous!" Ooh, that felt too harsh, but I continued. "There's way too much at stake. At some point we're all going to die. Maybe tomorrow. Maybe fifty years from now. Given what's at stake, why wouldn't you believe if you were at least 51% convinced it was true? To refuse to believe in God unless you have no doubts is …foolishness!"

I felt like I made a great point, but I didn't feel good about the conversation. An inner voice was telling me, *you're trying to win a debate rather than the person.* Is that something I heard Dad say? Was it a distant memory that surfaced from my subconscious.

"If you're going to make extraordinary claims, then you need extraordinary evidence."

"Not really. If natural explanations don't fit the evidence, and God is the best explanation, why not be open to that being the truth?"

"We have more important problems right now Lucy!" Mack's eyes were fierce. "I don't want Eli to be distracted with insanity."

Another insult. First nonsense. Now insanity.

"So, I'm insane?" I snapped.

"No. Your ideas are insane," Mack pointed at me.

"Just weeks ago, that is exactly what I used to think." The ferocity in his face melted away. "But I opened my mind to explore the truth. And I didn't have an unrealistic standard, like complete certainty or no doubts at all."

I turned to Eli, who was staring at me with a slight grin. He seemed to be enjoying the conversation. I ignored his father's glare. "With our eternal destination at stake, there's nothing more important than the truth about God, and accepting Jesus as our Lord and Savior. Not everyone needs evidence, many people don't; but it's certainly there for those who seek it, like me."

"I do believe in God," Eli said. "But I definitely don't know as much as you. I want to hear more."

"Really?" Mack snapped.

"Okay. Okay," Ruth interjected. "We all have different opinions." She held her hands out at her husband, as if trying to calm him down. He breathed heavy, as if releasing steam, decompressing his anger.

After several minutes, I felt my emotions begin to calm. Ruth and Eli broke the awkward silence with some banter about the taste of the capybara. Then I started to worry whether I'd been too aggressive with my verbal attacks. What if Mack had gotten angry enough to ditch me and Peter? My mouth could have gotten us into big trouble. I don't think he would do that, nor would Eli allow it. But I decided I had failed in my attempt to share truth. I recalled Dad's notebook mentioning it was one thing to know spiritual truth, but it needed to be shared in a gentle, respectful manner. I felt sad inside. A failure. I still believed I was right about having a realistic standard for determining spiritual truth, but I committed to doing better the next time I shared my convictions.

As I gazed at the flickering flames, a wave of fatigue swept over my body. I had not slept well the past few days. A string of dangerous situations had emptied my adrenaline and drained my emotions. Combined with all the physical exertion, I was beyond exhausted. I politely excused myself, entered the jeep and settled next to my brother. I closed my eyes and was asleep in minutes.

NINE

The birds seemed to be chirping extra loud this morning, as if releasing suppressed energy. I assumed they must have hunkered down last night during a severe storm. Thunder had shaken the jeep a few times, at least it felt that way to me; and water pelted the roof and windows. As tired as I had been, it woke me and kept me from falling back asleep for a while. Each crackle of thunder rattled my nerves. I remember thinking how fortunate Peter and I were for being protected in the jeep, rather than enduring the storm in some makeshift shelter. Eventually, I got a few more hours of sleep before morning arrived.

I sat outside of the jeep next to Peter, as Mack and Eli removed the vehicle's four tires. The surrounding area was drenched from the storm. The air was already warm, but also thick with humidity, surely countering evaporation in the wet jungle. I could see water dripping off leaves, splashing small puddles. But the drops were not audile; rather it was the squawking birds all around us that harassed my sanity. Thankfully, Peter and I were no longer alone.

Ruth handed me and Peter a delicious breakfast – Brazilian Tapioca Crepes. It was folded like a taco and filled with bananas. I prayed to myself, thanking God for meeting this family and providing this food. I believed it was truly an answer to prayer.

While I was happy to have last night's meal, this crepe was more to my liking. It was bland, but I enjoyed the sustenance of the carbohydrate; combined with sweet bananas and sugar, it was the best thing I had eaten in weeks, even better than the cheesy bread.

I washed it down with several gulps of guarana juice, which had a tangy apple-like taste.

"You still okay?" I asked Peter.

"No. The pain is too much," he said, as he chewed on a crepe. "I feel myself losing consciousness...probably slipping into a coma," his tone dripping with sarcasm.

"That's good. We won't need to feed you on the way home," I countered with my own wit. It's the second time I asked him this morning, and more and more, I had come to realize how much I cared about my brother. Maybe he had blocked out last night's trauma, but I will never forget his screams of agony. Fortunately, Ruth gave him a pill to relieve the pain and help him sleep.

I glanced down at his foot again. It certainly looked to be in a better position, but not exactly right. Still a bit crooked. Who knows if the bones are lined up correctly, but at least it's all tied securely in place.

Within an hour, Mack had built a cart for Peter to ride on. Two bamboo sticks were used as axles, placed between the center holes of the jeep's front and rear tires. These axles were connected eight feet apart by a bamboo stick on either side of both tires, forming a rectangle box. All were tied together with nylon rope, tight enough to hold the bamboo in place, but allowing the tires to rotate. Eight pieces of bamboo were then tied down as the base for Peter to sit on, along with all the supplies the family had packed, several large bags of food and water, as well as two backpacks of survival gear. With two ropes tied to the front axle, we took turns, two by two, pulling the cart.

Little was said as we journeyed along the dirt road. Periodically, Peter would give a slight whimper as movement and bumps jostled his foot. I could tell he was trying to refrain from revealing his discomfort, but I was sure the pain was too sharp to ignore. Unfortunately, Ruth didn't have any more pain relievers to offer. I could see the grimaces on his face; but he didn't complain once.

It was hard work pulling the cart, but the alternative of trying to carry Peter and all the supplies would have been near impossible. Eli and I were a team. I felt myself wanting to prove myself, pulling hard to make sure my side stayed even with his. The hills were the worst; even slight inclines were taxing given the weight of the cargo. Mack helped us on the inclines by pushing from the back.

Every fifteen minutes we rotated the teams pulling the cart; and we took full breaks after an hour. We all kept watch for danger, with either Mack or Eli carrying the rifle, in case a predator emerged. I noticed Mack continuously scanning the area to the right, presumably looking for the marina. The jungle was dense, but periodically the ocean could be seen between the trees, maybe three hundred yards away.

After three hours, we stopped for lunch. Nothing extraordinary. Granola, nuts and more fruit. But it was enough to replenish our energy.

As we resumed, a light rain sprinkled on us for a few minutes and then dissipated, just enough to be refreshing, but not get soaked.

After another hour of pulling, we reached a perpendicular dirt road to our right. There it was – the marina! A small two-story building, covered with heavily peeling white paint, was positioned close to the riverbank. Three long, wooden docks extended into the ocean; they were twisted and missing a couple planks. The dense jungle sandwiched the marina, close to either side of the docks.

There were several boats, including a couple large sailboats. But my heart sank when I recognized the largest boat. It was the skipper's boat, the one who had stolen our food a month ago, when we were lost at sea.

"Peter? Is that the skipper's boat?" I asked for confirmation.

"Yeah," he responded softly, with a hint of dread.

"What is it?" Mack asked.

I explained the previous encounter; how he pulled a gun on us, stole our food, and left us to die at sea.

"Everyone stay here," Mack ordered.

"No Dad. I'm coming," Eli pleaded, obviously not wanting his father to approach any danger without help.

"No!" Mack said harshly. "I need you to stay here and watch over everyone else."

Eli relented, either due to his Dad's glare that he had probably seen countless times, or perhaps because the task of protecting the rest of us made sense. Eli nodded and Mack gave him a handgun. I assumed that was the only other gun; otherwise, he would have given one to Ruth. Did she not like handling guns? Eli did seem to be more comfortable. I watched him check the ammunition and click the safety off.

Mack nodded to his wife, as if everything would be okay. He took the rifle in hand and slowly walked down the dirt road toward the marina. The way in which he advanced was cautious, staying alert. His head swiveled back-and-forth, obviously scanning for potential danger. I could see windows on the side of the house and back. A staircase in the back of the building led to a door on the second floor.

I scanned the area around me, jungle on either side of the dirt road. Should I try to push the cart into the jungle, hiding Peter and our supplies? I decided against it, hoping it wouldn't be necessary.

Mack arrived at the marina and peaked in a side window. Apparently not seeing anything interesting, he crept toward the front. As he reached the corner, a loud barking erupted. Angry growls and thundering barks indicated a large dog was outside.

I recalled the German Shepherd from the skipper's boat. My heart sank. I had forgotten it and failed to warn Mack. I was only focused on the sinister skipper and his gun.

Mack jumped back and pointed his gun, but after a moment seemed to relax. The barking continued, but it became obvious that Mack wasn't concerned. Perhaps it was tied up or in some sort of pen.

Rather than continue to the front door, Mack reversed course and circled around to the back steps that lead to the second floor. He crept up the staircase, looking into windows as he ascended. Mack listened at the door, then slowly turned the knob and entered the building. The barking finally ceased.

We all waited, not making a sound, listening for voices or signs of a struggle. Seconds turned into minutes. What could be taking so long?

"I'm going down," said Eli.

"No," Ruth grabbed his arm.

"Dad could be in danger!" Eli snapped. There was no questioning his courage.

Suddenly, the rear door opened, and Mack exited. He gave a thumbs up and made his way back to us. I continued to survey the area until he arrived, nervous about where the skipper might be. Was he hiding? Was he gone?

"No signs of any people," Mack informed us. "I checked the entire house and also scanned the outside from the second floor windows. I didn't see anybody. The dog is chained up near the front door."

After considering our options, we decided to take the largest sailboat. The skipper's boat would obviously be faster, but how far could we get with limited gas? We considered trying to bait the dog into the building, so its barking wouldn't attract attention, but decided it was better to just load the boat and get out of here, avoiding the angry canine.

Ruth and I pulled the cart, while Mack and Eli kept watch, their guns in ready position. As our small group reached the front of the marina, the booming barks erupted again. As we slowly passed the front, we were within twelve feet of the building. I was closest to the angry animal and got a good look at it.

The large dog was ferocious, and loud. Its menacing eyes glared at us as it snapped its jaws, snarling and revealing its sharp teeth. It yanked at its chain, desperate to attack us.

Suddenly the chain snapped. My eyes popped wide-open, and I froze, paralyzed with fear. The dog sprinted, closing the gap in a couple seconds and leaped at me. Instinctively, I raised my arms to protect my face. I felt a sharp bite on my right arm. The teeth immediately penetrated my skin, and the pressure was immense.

I heard multiple screams, "Lucy!"

The dog easily knocked me down and landed on top of me, still gripping my arm in its jaw. I began to fight it, punching at its snout with my left fist and flailing my legs to get it off me. Within a couple seconds, the dog was pushed off of me to the side, and I realized someone had shoved it.

I saw Eli lying on the ground next to me. I expected to get bitten by a counterattack from the aggressive animal. But it didn't come.

I heard barking and picked my head up to see Mack dragging the beast away by the portion of the chain that remained connected to its collar. It gnashed its teeth at me, as if desperate for another bite. Eventually it turned on Mack, but he smacked the dog and then hurled it inside the marina, before slamming the door shut.

Ruth was at my side, "Lucy? Are you okay?" She grabbed the open wounds on my arm. I yelped from the pain, but I knew she was securing the gashes. I looked over my shoulder at Peter, still sitting on the makeshift wagon. He looked into my eyes. "Are you alright?" he asked. I smiled and gave a thumbs up with my left hand to reassure him. I pulled myself up to a sitting position.

Ruth turned to Eli. "Are you okay?" He nodded, indicating he was fine, but he clearly looked shaken by the attack.

Mack ran back to us and grabbed a backpack off the cart. He opened it and removed a brown bottle. Eli got to his feet and joined his mother in consoling me. As he put his arm around my shoulders, I realized my body was shaking.

"Povidone-iodine?" Ruth asked. Mack nodded and poured it on my arm. I expected it to sting, but it didn't. Ruth then rinsed my arm with water, dried and bandaged it. While it was sensitive to touch – it felt heavily bruised – the injury didn't seem too bad, all things considered.

While I took a moment to calm down, it occurred to me that if it had it gotten to my neck, I could have died. Had God protected me from it being worse? Was I lucky? I couldn't know; but I was thankful, especially for Mack and Eli. Peter was visibly rattled by the attack. I could tell it bothered him that that he wasn't able to help me while I was being assaulted.

We took a few minutes to gain our composure. Mack kept guard, clearly worried the skipper could arrive at any time. Had he left the area? Was he dead? Who knows. I noticed Mack holding the gun tightly. He told us he almost shot the dog when it landed on me but hesitated just as Eli was leaping at the animal. When Eli shoved the dog, it got pushed into Mack, and it was easier for him to grab the chain rather than try to step back, aim and fire, at which point the dog could have charged at me or Eli.

Eli held me tight, his arm around my shoulders. His embrace brought comfort, and I felt my nerves settling.

"We should move," Mack said after a short time. Eli stood up; he extended a hand and helped get me to my feet.

Eli gave the handgun to Mack, who tucked it in the back of his jeans. Ruth and Eli picked up the ropes and began pulling the cart. I walked alongside, gently holding my injured arm, reassuring myself I would be okay.

We reached the docks with the cart but decided they were too dilapidated to pull it across. Mack and I helped Peter hobble over to the largest sailboat and get on board. It looked to be twenty-five feet in length and in good shape, from what I could tell. I helped Peter settle on a seat in the boat but sitting outside. I noticed steps that lead to a room inside, with a good amount of seating. It looked perfect for what we needed.

As we took turns bringing our supplies to the boat, Mack made his way over to the skipper's boat and looked inside. I wondered if he was looking for the skipper or any gear to take. When we finished with the supplies, Ruth stayed with Peter as Eli and I walked over to Mack.

"Anything worth taking Dad?" Eli asked.

"That would be stealing!" a raspy voice startled me. The three of us turned, to see the skipper had stepped out from behind a tree, close to the boat, with gun aimed directly at Mack.

TEN

I recognized the gun the skipper held as the one he aimed at my father a month ago.

"Drop it...or I shoot," the skipper said coldly. I noticed his angry glare and a twitch of his right eye.

Mack gently placed the rifle on the ground and slowly raised his hands.

I remembered that Mack had a gun tucked in his jeans behind his back. If I could divert the skipper's attention, perhaps it would give Mack a chance to take control of the situation. Should I ask the skipper a question to distract him? My heart was pounding, butterflies in my stomach. It would be a bold move. I gathered the courage to do it. *Be brave.* I told myself. *Be smart but be brave.*

"And the gun behind yur back," the skipper said, grinning slyly, nodding his pistol at Mack.

Ahhh! Somehow the skipper must have seen Mack's handgun. How long had he been watching us from the jungle?

"Turn around," the skipper ordered. "Remove the gun slowly and without turning back around, toss it toward me."

I studied the skipper's face. His jaw was tense. Cheeks rigid. Eyes cold and calculating. His deep wrinkles showed his age.

I turned my head to Mack, who complied, rather slowly, perhaps looking for a way to counter our opponent. But Mack finished by tossing the gun to the ground a few feet in front of us and stood with raised hands. My heart sank. Now what?

"We don't want trouble," Mack said, turning back to face the skipper. "We just want to leave."

"With one of my boats?" the skipper bellowed. "Not without paying for it." Were the boats really his, I wondered. It didn't matter.

"What do you want?" Mack asked. "How about you keep the rifle? Let me take the handgun for protection."

"Wait," the skipper squinted at me. His eyes seemed to be studying my face. "I recognize you." He nodded and smiled. "Yeah… You were in the raft a few weeks back. And that must be yur brother over there." He waved the gun at the sailboat. "But where's your Dad? Died on the raft?" He snickered. "Got eaten by a predator?" He chuckled loudly at his heartless joke.

I felt my body temperature skyrocket at the mention of my father. It seemed as though my blood was boiling, coursing through my body, burning my arteries. The rage I felt inside smothered all the nervousness I had felt. Instinctively, I stepped forward, wanting to strike him.

The skipper turned the gun on me, "I'll shoot ya," his face turned serious, and his right eye twitched, again.

"Please. These are kids," Mack said calmly, perhaps trying to defuse the tension. "You keep the rifle. Let us go."

"Yur not close to a deal," the skipper gruffed. "I want both guns…" He hesitated, then released a disturbing grin, "…and the girl and her brother stay with me. Yur not their father. You can go." He let out a full smile, showing his yellow teeth, triggering a flood of memories from the raft encounter with Peter and Dad. I remembered the skipper faking assistance, threatening us and feigning he would shoot us even after Dad gave the food.

Suddenly, I recalled that the skipper's right eye had twitched when he aimed the gun at my father, and then dropped it to his side. It was the same twitch he did again today, twice.

"There's no way anyone is staying with you," Mack sneered back at him. "I'm not leaving the kids behind." It should have melted my heart that Mack was standing up for me and Peter, but I was still furious that the skipper had mentioned my father.

I think he's bluffing, I said to myself. *His right eye twitches when he's bluffing. But what if you're wrong?* I countered myself. *Be courageous,* I told myself. *Be smart but be courageous!*

"I will shoot ya," the skipper sneered at Mack. His right eye twitched again.

"No…you won't," I said coldly stepping forward again, within ten feet. I dared not suggest aloud that he was bluffing, just in case I was wrong. It was my educated guess. "What's your name?" I asked.

"Lucy don't," Mack snapped.

"Lucy," Eli said, in a worried tone.

I extended my hand behind me for both of them to be quiet and gave Mack a nod and *trust-me* look; whether he understood or not, I don't know. His eyes narrowed, as if trying to understand what I was doing.

"Yur not in position to ask questions," the skipper growled. The words struck a chord inside me. It was a similar rebuttal he said to my father a month ago, again triggering my anger at the skipper.

"What's your name?" I repeated. I kept my voice calm and confident. I was seething inside, but I had a plan. We stared at each other for what felt like twenty seconds, but in reality, was probably ten.

"Victor," he said, grinning. "Nice to meet cha."

"You don't want to shoot anyone Victor," I said in an even-keel tone, shaking my head. "You know that threatening us is wrong. You should seek God and ask for forgiveness." The skipper gave a dismissive snicker, while I continued. "But shooting someone? That's another level, and deep down I don't think you want to shoot unless you really have to. And today, you don't have to. We will leave the rifle and a little food on the dock for you, as payment for the boat. But we're leaving. My father is dead. My brother is hurt badly. We're leaving. I'm leaving."

I stepped forward, picked up the barrel of the handgun and slowly raised it, showing it was not in position for me to fire it. I turned and started to walk away. I was confident in my assessment, but I didn't know for certain. I worried any second a blast would end my life.

But after a few steps, the skipper hollered, "Half the food."

"No!" I yelled turning back to face him. "There are five of us." I watched Mack and Eli start to take steps away. Mack's attention was focused sharply on the skipper. I turned again and continued to leave.

Slowly our distance from the threat increased, and the skipper dropped the gun to his side, a clear sign of relenting. We made our way to the docks and onto the sailboat, leaving a small bag of food, following through with my commitment.

No one said a word. Eli unhooked the rope from the dock and Mack raised the sail. I sat next to Peter, who gave me a puzzled look, "You're insane sis. You barely survived a dog attack..." *That's an exaggeration,* I thought to myself. "...and then you stare down a gun-wielding madman? Are you trying to get killed?"

"I don't want to die," I said softly. "But now I'm not afraid of it... like I used to be."

When a breeze took the sail, we started to slowly leave the dock. Ruth sat next to Eli and hugged her son. By her quivering, I could tell she had been terrified.

As we got about a hundred yards away from the docks, Mack looked back at the marina and then over at me. "I was wrong about you Lucy, in more ways than one. Your courage...is impressive."

After a fair amount of sailing, the land behind us had vanished from sight. There was little talking. Mack was focused on sailing, while the rest of us ate a good portion of granola and fruit, then rested. Peter was lying down on a cushion inside the boat. Ruth, Eli and I sat on benches outside. Mack wanted his wife and son to see what he was doing and listen to his explanations of basic sailing. At some point, they'd need to take-over to give him a break. I appreciated the warmth of the sun, a nice change from the wet jungle.

It felt surreal, leaving Brazil and all the trauma we had encountered. But as I closed my eyes, in hopes of sleeping, memories of floating at sea in the raft a month ago flooded my mind. The smell of salt water that I had grown to associate with the dangers of the sea was noticeable. The terrible anxieties I had felt, aimlessly drifting in the ocean, returned, rattling my peace. I needed to keep my eyes open as a reminder I was not in the same precarious situation. I was so tired of being anxious. I was physically and mentally drained.

Deciding I needed a change of scenery, I made my way inside the sailboat. Peter was lying on the couch to the left, his right foot resting next to the wall, with his left foot hanging off the couch, braced against the floor, probably to keep himself from moving. His eyes were closed, but apparently he heard me.

"Who's there?" he asked.

"Your sister. You dork," I answered playfully.

"Can't be. She wouldn't be that nice." He smiled at his corny response; eyes still closed.

I laid down on the opposite couch, but kept my eyes open, not wanting to drift back to memories of the raft. Our heads faced forward, in the direction the boat was headed.

I could hear the waves slapping against the side of the boat, and the water flowing underneath us. My imagination started to consider some terrifying realities. Beneath us was hundreds, if not thousands, of feet of water. Dark. Intimidating. Filled with sea creatures. Our very lives were protected by mere inches of wood, or fiberglass; whatever material it was. What would we do if we started to sink?

Why am I always thinking about worst case scenarios? I decided to close my eyes and give sleep another try. But I went right back to awful memories at sea.

"How are you able to rest?" I asked. "I can't get the raft out of my head."

"I don't know. I just don't think about it," he muttered.

"Not even the shark?"

"I guess...Honestly, I was more angry at the skipper. I was so mad when he took our food and left us."

"Hmmm," I mutter.

After a few seconds, Peter continued. "Kinda ironic that we have one of his boats now. That's karma."

"No such thing Peter," I said nonchalantly. I placed my arm over my eyes, hoping that would help me relax.

"Why not?" his tone perked up a bit. "I kinda like the idea of 'what goes around comes around'."

"Did you ever think it might be God's providence, taking care of us through natural laws? Or maybe it's just a coincidence," I said with a yawn. "Karma is not real."

"I like the idea of karma and reincarnation. Another chance. You know, to do better in the next life."

I couldn't tell if Peter really believed these things or was just trying to get a rise out of me. "It won't work Peter. You're not gonna get me all worked up. I'm too tired and happy to be leaving Brazil. Besides, reincarnation is not real. There are no good reasons to believe there's some invisible account tracking our good and bad deeds that determine what we are reincarnated as?"

"I don't care if you disagree. I kinda like the idea of karma and mixing it with Christianity."

"Peter! Now you're getting to me." I sat up and looked over at Peter. "Just because you like something that doesn't make it true!"

"Wow. I wasn't even trying to annoy you," he said with a chuckle. "I'm good at this younger brother thing."

"What do you mean mix it with Christianity? We don't get to pick what we like and decide spiritual truth?" My frustration was growing. I cared too much for my brother for him to go astray from the truth. I used to be self-absorbed, only focused on myself; but Dad's death seemed to change something inside – a desire to care about other people.

"Where do we really get spiritual truth?" he questioned, as if trying to sound like a deep thinker.

"Really? Don't you remember what Dad told us about the Bible? It is the Word of God – the written authority and source of spiritual truth. There is no other religious book like it. He gave reasons to believe it must be divinely inspired. Numerous fulfilled prophecies. Sixty-six books written over 1,500 years by about 40 authors, but one unified message about the salvation for human beings, which means it must have been directed by a divine author.[32] All that stuff ring a bell?"

"I guess so."

"You weren't listening, were you?"

"Of course I was…Maybe a little…Not really."

We both took a breath. Silence fell upon the inside of the boat. Again, I could hear the water flowing underneath the boat. Chilling.

"Wow. You've changed Lucy. You're like a whole different person in a month. Didn't you say the Bible is an ancient book that is no longer relevant?"

"Believe me – I'm surprised at how much I've changed. I've been thinking about this stuff for a long time from a negative perspective. But once I opened my mind, it just clicked, and all made sense. By-the-way, just because the Bible was written centuries ago, that doesn't make it false. That reasoning doesn't follow."

"You defending the Bible. I never would have guessed it."

"I hate to say it, but Dad dying made me care about this stuff. Who is God? What are human beings? How do we get to heaven? The Bible is where we get the truth about the most important questions.[33]"

"So maybe the Bible includes reincarnation," Peter offered.

"No. Dad's notes mentioned Hebrews 9:27, which says we die once, and afterward face judgment."

"I don't know Lucy. I read that some Christians believe in reincarnation."

"I know but that doesn't make it true. People can have wrong beliefs. You need to check the Bible."

"Sure, but people interpret it differently."

"Right. So, you should read it yourself; and if something is not clear, research good interpretations…And don't trust everything on the internet. I've started to realize we need to be very careful about the sources where we get our information. It's so easy to read false things about religion, about politics, about our identity as human beings, and we just assume it's true. We get taken captive by lies and don't even know it."

"If they're lies, just ignore them," Peter said matter-of-factly.

"Sounds easy, but it's not. Dad wrote that sometimes lies are mixed with elements of truth or nice words, making them harder to notice and easier to accept.[34]"

"So, I have a few lies bouncing around in my head. Who cares?"

I couldn't tell if Peter was trying to get under my skin. Despite my efforts to resist, it was working. His last statement bothered me; I didn't want my brother believing lies. Just recently I realized I had lived a lot of my life being held captive by lies about myself. I felt like the truth about Jesus set me free.[35]

"It's important," I responded. "I now realize that our ideas, the things we believe, are critical. They shape who we are and what we do.[36]"

"Wow. Lucy the philosopher."

"Peter. Are you listening to what I'm sharing?" my voice was elevated.

"I thought you weren't going to get worked up," he said with a smile.

"I'm not," I said, trying to convince myself. I laid back down. "Just…This is really important. I…can't bear the thought of us not all being together in heaven."

"How are we going to tell Mom about Dad?"

The question hit me hard. I hadn't even thought about that. For the first time in a few weeks, I wasn't consumed with my own despair or survival.

"I don't know," I managed to say.

"It'll crush her."

"I know. But she'll be happy we're okay." I felt like I was trying to console Peter a bit.

We both let the conversation fade to silence. I felt myself beginning to doze; then startled awake. I don't know how long I was sleeping before I was awoken by Mack yelling.

"Ruth! Ruth, we might have trouble!"

I jumped up from the couch and staggered on hands and feet to the outside portion of the boat. The sun was bright. I saw Ruth standing, facing the front. She shielded her eyes from the sun with her hand. "What is it?" she asked nervously.

Mack pointed straight ahead. "Looks like a military patrol boat speeding this way."

I stood and peered in the direction Mack had pointed. A small craft in the distance was quickly approaching, bouncing along the waves. A faint hum from their engine was getting louder.

"Let me do the talking," Mack said. I wonder if that command was intended for me, as if I had grown bold enough to try to take over the situation.

Within minutes a military speed boat arrived. A heavy machine gun was anchored in the front, with a soldier aiming it at our boat. Three other soldiers, that I could see, were in the boat. One driving. One armed with a rifle. And one, who appeared to be leading them, held a megaphone in his hand.

"This is the U.S. Navy. You are not allowed to proceed. You must return to Brazil."

My heart sank. This was horrifying de ja vu. The last time we tried to leave Brazil, it was in a plane, but we were forced to return. A month later, the country was undoubtedly in even tighter lock down.

"Wait," Mack held up his hands. "My name is Mack Pruitt. I'm a contractor for the Pentagon. We are all American citizens. Please call Lieutenant General Allard."

"I don't care who you are or who you claim to know. I have orders. Nobody leaves. I'm sorry to all of you, but you must return."

The words shattered my spirit. It would be crushing to have to go back. And do what? Build a shelter? Go back to the cabin? Try to wait out the horrible virus?

"I'm pleading with you," Mack held out his hands. "Please. Just place a call."

The soldier shook his head and said something to the solider next to him. They dialoged for a minute, before the leader picked up a transmitter. I could see him talking for a while and then place it down.

"I radioed back to the ship," the leader called out to us. "Now we wait."

I told Peter what happened and then made my way over to a seat outdoors, eager to hear the response. The soldiers with the heavy gun and rifle stayed alert, watching us intently.

Mack left the steering wheel – 'helm' I think he called it – and walked over to Ruth. "If this doesn't work, were gonna be in trouble."

Eli stood up and approached me. His eyes trained on my face, perhaps seeing how distraught I felt.

He sat next to me. "No matter what happens, I won't leave you and Peter."

"Thank you," I whispered. His words were beyond reassuring. I instinctively placed my head on his shoulder and grabbed his arm. I relished his confidence and unwavering care. He made me feel valued and safe.

After a long thirty minutes, the leader of the military craft startled me with his megaphone. "Mr. Pruitt?" Mack stood, facing the solider. "I have a response. You will be coming with us. We will throw a rope to you and tow you back to the destroyer. You will wait on your vessel for one week, while we give you food and water. After that time, our medical personnel will conduct tests on you. If all is okay, you will be allowed to board the ship."

"Thank you…Thank you," Mack repeated, releasing a heavy sigh of relief.

A mix of emotions sprang up from within. I felt a jolt of excitement. I was grateful to finally be heading home. But I also had an empty feeling going back without Dad. I clung tighter to Eli's arm. I knew we were much better off going home, but the world was still facing a tremendous danger.

CHAPTER
ELEVEN

U.S. – about 15 years later

"So that's how you met Dad," Zach beams.

I smile back at him, "Yeah. That's how I met your father. He was very brave. Just like you," I say with a playful punch to his arm. I feel butterflies stirring in my stomach. Reminiscing has left me more emotional than I want. I need to focus on today's task. I decide to suppress the memories. Subdue my emotions.

Zach stares off in the distance, as if deep in thought. "That's why Uncle Peter limps," he says softly.

"Yeah," I confirm, realizing I never explained all this to him. I'm sure Peter told Zach his foot got injured, but I guess he never gave details. Can't blame him for not wanting to relive the trauma.

I'm very disappointed Peter isn't able to be here today. I could really use his support; but he clearly got food poisoning last night. It was early evening when he got violently sick, cramping and vomiting for hours. Unfortunately, it's not unusual in today's world. We try to preserve food as best as possible, but sometimes meat spoils quickly. Luckily, Zach and I ate something different and are fine. Peter was stable this morning; weak and dehydrated, but I'm confident he'll be okay.

"But what else?" Zach begs, clearly wanting more. "You didn't say how you got home."

I shrug my shoulders. "There really isn't much more that's exciting about getting home. We were towed to a warship. They

Jason M. Jolin

quarantined us in the sailboat for a week to make sure we weren't sick." As I say the words, I'm sad to realize that Zach, at eight years old, lives in a world where he knows exactly what quarantine means. "Then they did some medical tests on us and let us aboard. We had to stay on the ship for a few weeks until another ship was heading home, and we got a ride."

I didn't want to go into what happened after we arrived at America. D63 had just reached U.S. soil. We were ushered off the ship. Chaos ensued in the country. Travel was a nightmare. It took me and Peter a long time to get home; by then, our immediate family had passed. Our mother and three older siblings were among the early victims. Peter and I never got to see them before the awful disease took them from us.

Again, I choose to compartmentalize the painful memories. I need to concentrate on today's objective.

I look around to make sure no wildlife has found its way into the football field. I know it's unlikely, especially with the fencing, but I just need to make sure. Nothing.

Zach is picking grass out of the ground, apparently getting bored with waiting. I say a brief prayer in my mind, asking God to help me speak confidently to all who are coming. My hope is we will all decide to come together as one large community, not only to unite against the danger, but to reduce the degree of seclusion.

I have often thought the state of the world is so contrary to what God desires – people are designed to be relational, not isolated. I understand why we live in separation, but it torments me. I wish there was a way to return to how things were when people were able to interact and have close relationships. Although my mind knows it's dangerous and foolish, my heart yearns for that dream scenario. Zach doesn't know any different, but I remember a different world; and I pray for it – often.

After a short time, I see the first person emerge from the tree line. It's Dario, followed by his parents, Juan and Maria. Dario, who is in his early fifties, is one of my favorite people in our community. Hardworking. Trustworthy. Quiet, but dependable. His parents are good

102

people too. Of all the families I have met, they are the most willing to share all of their resources with the rest of our community, which is unusual in this world. They are Christians, like my family. Dario points to me and speaks something in Spanish to his parents. They all know English but seem more comfortable conversing with each other in Spanish. I recall the pain Dario shared when he lost his wife and daughters to the disease.

Leo and Phoebe arrive next, with their five-year old daughter, Esther. I'm pleasantly surprised. I thought only one of them would come, with the other staying home with their little one. She was born a couple years after D63 sprang its horror on the world. What a terrible way to begin a family. Esther looks like a little version of her Mom – long blond hair with natural waves. They are easily the youngest family in our community, with the parents being in their late twenties. Phoebe is currently pregnant, five or six months, I think.

Tabitha arrives right after the young family. She's in her early fifties. My heart breaks for her. She lost her mother to the horrible disease about a year ago, and now lives alone. After being bitten by a wolf, her mother quarantined herself in their garage. We prayed and hoped the wolf didn't have the virus...but it did. The suffering her mother experienced crushed Tabitha; it changed her from someone who was a happy extravert to a depressed loner. While she is my height and build, short and thin, she looks a lot like her mother. With a mix of some Hawaiian descent, her complexion has a slight tan, and she has long, wavy black hair. Her house is closest to mine, which led to our developing a bond. We were once best friends. But since her Mom passed, she has withdrawn from everyone, and our relationship has faded. I'm glad she came today.

Sophia and Nathan arrive next. They are brother and sister in their late forties. Nathan has down-syndrome; and unlike a couple other people with down-syndrome I have met who are cautious about what causes D63, Nathan is not careful. Many of us are surprised he has been able to survive in this harsh world, as he sometimes disregards his sister's rules. He's gotten bitten by a wild dog and scratched by a rooster, but no D63. He's either incredibly lucky or one of the very rare people in the world who is immune.

Gus arrives along with Ahmed. They're the oldest in our community, both in their late seventies, although Dario's parents are not far behind in age. Gus and Ahmed are neighbors who both lost their wives about the same time a decade ago, not related to the deadly disease. They are friends, but they routinely argue about everything. Gus is what one would call a 'curmudgeon' – a grumpy old man, who finds the negative in everything. He is of medium build, with thinning white hair and glasses. His raspy voice fits his grouchy demeanor.

Ahmed is a dark-skinned man, of middle eastern descent. He is a devout Muslim. He and I have discussed religion many times; and while he seems open to listening, he's been resistant to changing his views, so far. Of course, I'm sure he thinks the same of me. His demeanor is quiet, unless provoked by Gus saying or doing something that irks him. Then he rebukes Gus and the two begin to verbally jab each other. If you didn't know their routine, you might worry it would escalate to a physical altercation.

This is our entire community. Along with Peter, Zach and myself, we total fourteen people, soon to be fifteen. About seven years ago, we were a neighborhood of more than fifty people; but D63 transmissions exploded, partly due to infected mammals. The amount of people declined sharply. But it's not about numbers. I lament each life that was cut short; everyone who died had a personal story and left behind broken hearts. They have a soul that I hope is safe from eternal punishment.

After we exchange greetings, the other community arrives. They live in a small neighborhood about five miles away, in a slightly more wooded setting. My community is in a suburban development with houses on either side of the road. There are still trees between our houses, but the homes are more visible than the other community.

They are a group of twenty people among five large families. Unlike our community, they are mostly younger and tend to interact more readily. They are led by John Sato, who is a Japanese man in his sixties, the oldest of his group. He is small in stature – just about my height – but one of the smartest people I have met. He is a former CEO, trained in engineering and a grandmaster chess player. He organized the bartering of resources amongst his community and utilized everyone's talents to enable all to thrive. I have sought his counsel many times.

They are the only other group I have stayed in contact with since the latest peril I am about to discuss. Other communities I met years ago are more than a few days travel away, if they still exist.

After my community welcomes them, and we exchange pleasantries, they take a seat in the bleachers at the remaining cones. I wait for the chit chat to fade. Then I stand and hold my hands up to get everyone's attention. It doesn't take long, as they have all come to hear what I have to say.

"Thank you everyone," I say loudly. The lingering murmur quickly fades to silence. "Thank you all for coming. It's been a long time since our communities have come together. And I would not have asked you here today if it wasn't for a good reason."

I wonder what everyone's reaction will be. Has anyone already heard the news? My hope is we will decide to come together as one community, to all help each other confront this new danger.

"Many of you know that I keep in contact with other communities. Through those relationships, I have become aware of a new threat. A danger that gives me great concern that I need share with all of you." I pause and scan the crowd to ensure I have their attention. "People are being abducted…Either one at a time or whole families at once… The two communities to our East…are no longer there."

Facial expressions amongst both groups show a mix of shock, perplexion and anxiety. Clearly no one was aware. I continue.

"It began with the community near Baker's Lake. They had ten people, but all are gone. Either all abducted or maybe some fled. It started a few months ago when a couple of people went missing. While the community mourned, no one considered anything to be unusual. They all assumed those couple of people got sick or were attacked by a wild animal. The next time I went out there, the rest were missing."

I wonder how Zach is taking the news. I look down and see his eyes trained on me. Does he understand the magnitude? I delayed him hearing as long as I could; and then wanted to tell him last night, but Peter got sick. Today, I've been focused on what to say to these communities, knowing I have time on the way home to get his reaction and answer questions.

Suddenly, Gus calls out with his raspy voice, "Cannibals!"

People immediately begin to stir with fret. Cannibalism was folklore several years ago when perishable food was depleted and people were starving; but since the human population has dwindled and wildlife is plentiful, it hasn't been a concern for years.

"I don't think so," I quickly respond, trying to subdue that particular fear.

"How do you know Lucy?" Gus grumbles.

"Let her finish," Ahmed barks at him. They exchange annoyed looks at each other. I decide to interject before they continue to banter.

"I don't think it's cannibalism," I say, shaking my head and holding up a hand. "It seems the abductors want these people for something. Let me finish sharing what I was told." Gus looks disgruntled, eyebrows pointed downward and nostrils flaring. It doesn't take much to stir his anger.

"A few weeks later, a second community, the one next to Baker's Lake, started to lose people. That's when we realized something different was happening. Our fears were confirmed when a young girl, hiding in her home in a cabinet close to a blazing fireplace, witnessed her uncle being abducted. She described the intruders as wearing rubber suits with masks. We assume they were medical hazard suits. The intruders fired some kind of dart to render the uncle unconscious. She saw them remove the dart and carefully carry his body. The way she described their being cautious with his body indicates they wanted him alive. That's when the remaining twelve people told me they were leaving the area."

106

It's eerily quiet. Everyone is obviously waiting for what's next.

"There are no other surrounding communities in close proximity," I say. "So, if more abductions continue, one of our communities is probably next." I feel relief in sharing this news. I've been carrying it for a couple days. Peter was the only one I had told.

I study John Sato's face. It's expressionless. Unreadable. Did he already know? He's smart. But unlike myself, he doesn't stay in contact with other communities. I wanted to tell him before today, but he was away hunting when I got this latest news about the girl witnessing her uncle. Perhaps he is already processing options, thinking through each alternative as a master chess player would do.

As if noticing I'm watching him, John Sato asks. "What are you suggesting we do Lucy?" It is as if leader is speaking to leader on behalf of their communities.

"Thanks for asking John," I make sure I speak the next words with confidence. "I think our communities should join together and prepare for this potential danger."

I see a wave of uneasiness spread through both groups. It has become common knowledge that whenever large groups of people have tried to coexist, a small contagion of the virus eventually ravages the community. It's too difficult to maintain strict guidelines. Impromptu human interaction is more prevalent with larger numbers; and, if one person gets infected without knowing, the virus can spread like wildfire.

I see John Sato rubbing his chin with his thumb and index finger, as if analyzing my recommendation. I decide to continue, making my case for all to consider.

"We all know it's easy to move to a new location, but not necessarily easy to survive. It's difficult to leave a functional place and make a new home with enough resources to live. Rain barrels to get plenty of water. An ample supply of wildlife to hunt or fish. Gardens and fruit trees for harvesting. No matter what we all decide, we face risk. But I'm convinced that uniting against this threat is our best alternative. We should help each other and not live in fear."

Gus points at me, "That's easy for you Lucy. At your age, if fighting doesn't work, you can flee this place in a hurry, easier than me."

"Gus. Do you really think this is an easy decision for me?" I counter, motioning to Zach. "In some ways, it feels safer for me with a child to leave."

In fact, there is nothing in this life that scares me more than losing Zach in this manner. The possibility of him being abducted, not knowing where he is – alive or suffering – it would crush me. I've already lost my husband, who five years ago didn't return from one of his scavenger trips. I don't know if he was ambushed by humans or attacked by wildlife. I searched for weeks but couldn't find him. He wasn't the only one; years ago, when there were more people on Earth, others didn't return from scavenger trips. Fighting over resources was far more common.

The emotional scar of my husband was reopened, like a fresh wound, when I heard about these recent abductions. I wanted to take Peter and Zach and run. Leave everyone else behind. But after agonizing over the situation and stopping to pray, I felt it was right to stay. I know most, if not all in my community, will not leave. Given their ages or situations, they probably won't feel like it's possible. I was tempted to justify my desire to leave as what is best to protect my son; but deep down I know I would simply be letting fear drive my decision. I simply cannot leave these people who have been there for me all these years.

John Sato asks, "Do they have a vehicle?"

"Yes," I confirm. "It seems they have an electric van. Very quiet."

Someone from John's community asks how joining together as one community would work? Not in a way to support or reject the idea, but I can tell it's out of curiosity.

From a safety perspective, it would be great to have John's community join ours. Not only are they younger, they have better weapons. Currently they use them for hunting, but the firearms would certainly be effective in self-defense.

But if I'm honest, I have also yearned for years to see a large community of people interacting. People living in isolation has been a burden on my heart. They are surviving, not thriving. They are just existing. I want to be safe given our circumstances, but I despise this world; not just that it's dangerous, but it has robbed us of relationships that are essential for human beings.

"If we decide to unite, your community could relocate to our neighborhood," I offer. "There are plenty of houses that have long been vacated and plenty of visibility to keep watch over everyone. We would implement strict protocols for limiting interactions and quarantine. But again, there are more of us to watch over and defend each other."

A man from John's community interjects, "Just because we would be close, it doesn't mean we'd be safer." The tone is clearly skeptical. "If we don't organize a defense, we're just a cluster of targets."

I think his name is Jared, but not being sure, I don't mention it. "It's a fair point. I was thinking we would prepare in a few ways. First, we would set up a lookout. We'll have a guard in the house closest to the main road that can watch all three roadways into our community. We'll have shifts that take turns watching the streets. If a vehicle is seen, we'll signal everyone to hide. We would then…"

"But Lucy…" Amara, a young woman from John's community interrupts. "How are we going to communicate with each other?" She is very smart and considered John's closest advisor.

I did forget to explain that before starting the next point. *Slow down Lucy*, I tell myself. "Good question Amara. Dario found several boxes of short-range radios at a distribution center, and a good supply of solar-powered batteries. There are more than enough for everyone. This is the way we would stay in contact."

Leo interjects, "But if there's a van approaching our community, is there really enough time to alert everyone and hide?"

"Good question Leo," I say. "One thing we need to do is slow down potential invaders by blocking each road. It may not stop them, but it should give us more time. This is step two of the plan. Cut down tall trees and push large objects into the roads to barricade them. Impede the potential intruder."

"But if there is an enemy out there and they spot a new barricade, won't that make them suspicious?" Phoebe asks.

"Maybe," I concede. "But I'm hoping it's an effective obstacle or deterrent. I want them to know we will protect ourselves.

"But you suggested hiding, right?" Tabitha asks. "Not fighting." My guess is she's not keen on combat.

"Yes. We don't know who is abducting people or why. How many there are. What weapons they have. Until we know more about this enemy, I don't think we should engage them unless we have to. If someone in our communities is being abducted, then we will all defend them with our lives."

Jared interjects again, "But if we have the element of surprise, wouldn't we want to ambush them?"

"We could," I answer. "I'm open to defending ourselves, but I wonder if we first avoid engagement and set traps until we know more about them."

Jared continues, "But if we're discovered and lose the element of surprise. It may be too late. If they are more powerful and know we're here, they'll just keep coming back."

"If we're discovered and we can't defend ourselves, we'll need to flee. This is the last part of the plan – have a contingency to vacate the area, if necessary." I go on to explain a couple possibilities for escape and ways we can defend ourselves if cornered or someone is at risk for abduction.

I see John Sato rubbing his forehead, as if mentally processing all I've shared. Then he finally speaks. "Lucy, are you aware of anyone engaging these abductors? Anyone who has successfully fought them off?"

"No," I have to be honest. "Attacks are random between day and night, but most times an abduction wasn't discovered until someone was missing. Other than the girl witnessing the men in hazard suits, it's been a bit of a mystery. That's why I don't know that we should engage them unless we need to."

Someone in John's group gets his attention and speaks softly to him.

John turns to his community and motions them together at the end of the bleacher, out of earshot. They are huddled together as a group – so much for them needing cones for spacing. It's clear they are having their own discussion. Families within my community start to chat as well. Everyone is digesting the news and sharing their reactions.

I'm not sure how to interpret what is happening. It's hard to read body language. Most seem bewildered, as if wondering if the news is real. I expected more panic, but perhaps the news is too raw. In fairness, I've known for longer.

After a short time, John Sato's group disburses, and turns to me. John speaks on their behalf. "Lucy. We want to thank you for sharing this information with us. You know I have great respect for you, and we all appreciate you and everyone in your community."

Uh-oh, I'm thinking. My sense is these compliments are meant to soften the blow of news I don't want to hear.

"But we have decided it's best for us to leave the area. We're not comfortable with a super-community. Honestly, we have been talking about leaving this area for a while. Moving south to a warmer place with more land to farm."

His response devastates me. *I failed,* is all I can think.

"Lucy," John says. "I hope our paths cross again."

And with that, John's community makes friendly good-bye gestures and they're off. I'm stunned; and very disappointed I was unable to convince everyone to come together. They didn't seem to consider the possibility with any seriousness. I thought there would be more discussion and then some kind of vote or something.

By the expressions of my community, they're surprised as well.

"We should leave too," Tabitha says. "Right?"

"I'm not leaving," Gus grumbles. "We don't even know if any danger is going to come here. It would be ludicrous to leave all we have."

"I can't leave Lucy," Ahmed follows. "I don't have it in my body."

"I don't think Nathan and I could leave," Sophia says, shaking her head. "We barely survive as it is."

Chatter breaks out amongst the families. Voices escalate as anxiety increases.

I hold up my hands, "Let's stay calm and talk about our options."

After the anxious jabbering subsides, each person takes turns sharing their opinions, some longer than others. Besides Tabitha, everyone either wants to stay, or feels it's necessary that they remain. Leo and Phoebe wrestled with it a bit, and reserved the right to change their mind, but they have spent a lot of time building a place to live, and with Phoebe in mid-pregnancy, they don't think right now is feasible. This is what I expected; the community as a whole, is not willing or able to move.

I still feel defeated by the decision of John's community. It wasn't much of a decision for them. But I keep telling myself I need to move forward, put aside this feeling of failure.

I notice everyone looking at me, as if waiting for my confirmation. I look down at Zach. His expression tells me he understands more than I would prefer. My heart desires to flee, but I have already prayed and decided.

I turn back to my community. "I will not leave you. We will not leave you," I say, looking down at Zach again.

"I don't need you Lucy," Gus says gruffly. "I will shoot any stranger I think..."

"Gus!" Ahmed hollers.

"I will!" Gus yells back.

"Guys!" I shout. "If we're not united, we're vulnerable."

"Lucy?" Dario interjects. "There's really no way to conceal we're living here. But I'm happy to help prepare us to fight."

"Thank you Dario," I can always depend on his support. "We have to assume this enemy is powerful. So, I think we should use our houses as a decoy. I suggest we live in a house next to our home, where there is a chair in front of the door. We will secure all entryways to our current home except for the front door, which will have a trap. So, if an enemy does invade our community, whether we know it or not, they'll trigger a trap. If nobody comes in the next few months, we can go back to our original home."

We talk about this idea for a while, and everyone agrees it's a good start. Leo asks about my plan to flee if necessary. I had mentioned some general ideas but had not shared one specific option that really only works for our community.

"If our plan doesn't work...if our hand is forced, and we must move, it would be better to take as many supplies as possible. My idea is to move some of our extra supplies and hide them in the two large catamaran sailboats at the marina. If danger comes that we can't handle, we could flee in the sailboats. Steer them far down the river to try to find a new location to live."

"There's enough room?" Ethan asks. "I don't know about being in a confined area."

I'm not surprised. I'm sure he's concerned about his family. "The boats are big," I answer. "Forty feet. I searched them for supplies years ago. Each of them has four cabins and room for supplies and animals. We can steer them down the river..."

"Still a big risk Lucy," Ethan interrupts.

"I hear you. There may be a smaller boat a family can take."

Gus breaks out in a ridiculing laugh. "This is an absurd idea. How do you know they aren't rotting? Or infested with rodents?"

I take a breath to resist snapping back. "Again...this is not the primary plan." I say, shaking my head. "We're going to prepare to stay. Defend our homes. But if we need to leave, we probably won't survive if we don't take supplies. Lots of them. This is the best idea I could think of to flee the area, with supplies and some of our animals. Walking out of here with supplies on our backs is a lot riskier."

I can see expressions are changing. Perhaps people are recognizing it's a viable option.

"I do think Gus brought up a good point," I agree, motioning to him. "And I would like to go and check out the catamarans tomorrow. Make sure they are structurally sound. Tabitha? Would you be willing to come with me?"

Her head jerks backward. Her eyes reveal her surprise at my suggestion, perhaps deep in other thoughts. Her father was a sailor, so she grew up around boats.

Jason M. Jolin

"I don't know," Tabitha shakes her head. "I'm still processing everything."

I could use her help, and I don't want to take Zach. But I'm not going to push. It's not the first time I've traveled alone.

We spend the next half-hour talking about the details of our plans. Which adjacent houses we'll temporarily live in? Who will take shifts in the lookout house? How will we block certain roads?

As we are breaking up and heading home, Tabitha looks my way. "I'll go with you tomorrow."

I'm surprised and grateful. "Great! I'll see you tomorrow morning at nine."

CHAPTER
TWELVE

I exit the back door of the house next to my home. It was the first night Peter, Zach and I slept in this house. But that's the plan for the foreseeable future; everyone in the community stays hidden at night in the house next door, while our homes, which clearly look inhabited, are the trap. My home doesn't have a trap inside the front door yet; Peter is going to work on that today. He also agreed to set one in Tabitha's house while she is with me.

The morning air is cold and bites at my face. I'm sure it won't take long for my nose and cheeks to turn pink. A wool hat protects my head from the chill, but I don't dare cover my ears, which could muffle hearing potential danger. I see the white of my breath and realize we are quickly approaching winter.

I make my way over to the coop and fencing that contains over thirty chickens. Most are standing still, as if frozen. Some periodically cluck. A few scratch at the ground, and eye the dirt for something to eat.

The coop was previously a large shed that Peter and I converted. We cut a hole in the side for chickens to enter and exit the shelter. Then we built a large area of wired fencing around the shed and added a wire mesh over the top to protect against birds of prey. Heavy-duty wire was added to the ground all around the outside perimeter to prevent predators from digging their way in to attack our primary food source.

Our chickens are essential to survival. They produce at least a dozen eggs a day, and older chickens not laying are slaughtered for food when we don't have meat from hunting or trapping, such as deer or squirrel. If something ever happened to these chickens, we could be in serious trouble.

Ten feet away is our cast iron hand pump to get well water. It's even more important than the chickens. Other than seven hand pumps attached to wells in the neighborhood, a small stream a half mile behind our house is the only natural water close to us. It's not only a lot of walking, it's dangerous to continuously travel deep into the woods. We only go that far back for hunting, and never alone.

These resources are a reminder it's not easy to just pick up and move. It's a lot of work to build a survival system that provides plenty of food and water. In addition to the chickens, we have a large garden, several traps to catch small game, and rain barrels attached to the gutters of our home, and both houses next to ours.

Today, Peter and Zach will finish moving some necessary supplies to our temporary home. Peter will then set a trap with a flash grenade. I have a monitor set up to hear if it goes off in the middle of the night. I need to rotate the solar batteries routinely to ensure they don't die, and we potentially miss a signal. Peter insists he'll take lead in fighting if a threat comes, but he just can't move well. We argue about this often. He's certainly stronger than me and a better shot, but his lame foot makes it difficult for him to move quickly.

Checking my solar-powered watch, it's time to begin today's mission. I make my way to the front of the house, heading for Tabitha's home, a couple houses down the street. While nocturnal predators should have withdrawn to their lair or den, you never know. There's always a chance danger is lurking. I left my rifle, choosing to take one of my pump shotguns for protection.

I stay alert as I make my way down the road. I scan for movement in the grass and bushes on either side of the road that has overtaken each yard, listening for rustling leaves. Thankfully, it's a relatively quiet morning. Despite many years in this new world, I have never gotten used to the sounds, which are virtually all natural. Wind blowing leaves, birds chirping, howls from wild dogs and an occasional wolf. Zach doesn't know any different, but I find it eerie.

While I'm physically moving forward, I'm still struggling emotionally with yesterday's decision by John's community. I had hoped both communities would decide to join together. Form a super-community. Would it have made us stronger to face a potential intruder? Absolutely. But I cannot ignore my desire for people to someday shed the shackles of isolation. We're not designed by God to live with such limited interaction. I understand it's been necessary for survival, but it's demoralizing. I have told myself to 'get over it' but I cannot shake my yearning for this dream.

The way I typically counter my disappointment is to keep my mind busy, trying to find ways to help people. Sometimes I've shared hope about going to heaven. Sometimes it's about helping my community survive or prepare for different scenarios. Admittedly, I'm not sure about our community potentially fleeing the area by boat. I'm not convinced it's viable…yet. But it's important to investigate all options.

I see Tabitha sitting on the steps of her home. It's a small two-story house, similar style to mine. She wasn't prepared to stay in the house next door but plans to do so tonight. A garage to the left of her home reminds me of the terrible death of her Mom – Ruth. Almost a year ago, she was bitten by a wolf who surprised her in the backyard. She has able to fight off the animal, but the damage was done. Tabitha witnessed the attack from a short distance away and ran to her mother. But her mother made her stay at a distance. She then quarantined herself in the garage, away from Tabitha; and unfortunately fell sick to D63.

The cries of Ruth experiencing the effects of the disease were horrific. I visited the outside of the garage every day, talking with her and then praying when she was experiencing a muscle tear. Tabitha was always with us, sitting somberly on the other end of the garage. I shared the hope of Jesus as the Savior for our sins. After a short time, she accepted Him as the truth and became a Christian.

After her mother passed, I tried to support Tabitha. But she withdrew and isolated herself, spending months in mourning. She barely did enough to survive. I know what that's like; but she wouldn't let me help her. Thankfully, she seems to slowly be returning to her natural disposition.

"Morning Tabitha," I say, holding up my hand.

"Hi Lucy," she responds with a grin. She gets to her feet and throws a backpack around her shoulders, onto her back. She makes her way over to me.

"How are you today?" I ask.

"I'm great," she responds with a big smile. "Looking forward to helping today." Her expression and words seem forced, as if trying to be convincing. Maybe she's just having a tough day and trying to hide it. Perhaps a memory of her mom. "How are you?" she asks.

I try to recall if she had the same disposition yesterday. I don't think so. Then I realize there's been a silent pause. "I'm good. Getting cold, huh?"

"Yeahhhhh!" she agrees, emphatically rubbing her arms with both hands. We both wear large flannel jackets, protecting our thin bodies; but unlike me, she doesn't have light armor on her forearms and shins. I suspect she probably gets cold like me this time of the year.

"Hopefully it'll get warmer during the day," I respond. "Ready to go?"

"Yes. Yes!" Again, her response seems more pressed than natural. Am I overanalyzing? Maybe. But I'm good at reading people.

We begin our trek to the marina, which is about three miles away. I expect it will take almost an hour. A slight breeze is in my face. Nothing to do but grin and bear the cold wind.

"When was the last time you were at the marina?" I ask.

"Oh...uh...long time. Maybe five years ago, Mom and I went back looking for supplies we thought might be there."

"Sorry. I didn't mean to bring up your mom."

"No. No, I...I'm coping okay now. I believe she's in a better place."

She seems sincere. Okay, I guess she's not having a tough day due to memories. I must be overthinking. That's not unusual for me.

"Did you bring food?" I ask. "I have plenty. Carrots. Apples. Some dried meat."

"Ha. Great minds think alike," she says pointing at her head. "I also have apples and carrots." We chuckle at what is a silly coincidence. That's her natural, light-hearted demeanor.

We are approaching the end of our road. To the left is Gus's house at the end of the road, but he is staying at the house next door, the one we just passed. To the right, across the street and also at the end of our road, is a two-story house we are calling *The Tower*. It is an empty house being used as the post for whoever is watching over the roads leading into our community. It provides good visibility of our street and the other street to the right of us where the rest of the members of our community lives. Both are dead ends, so this is good place to observe.

Next to the *The Tower* is Ahmed's home. Gus and Ahmed live diagonally across from each other. They have for decades. For the time being, both agreed to stay with each other in the house we just passed.

"I didn't see Gus or Ahmed," I say. "But they must be awake. Gus is an early riser." I force the thought out of my head that either could have been abducted.

Tabitha doesn't respond.

"What did you think of yesterday's meeting?" I ask.

"Hmm…" Her head drops a bit, eyes at the ground. I can tell immediately that her disposition has changed again. Maybe she has changed her mind and wants to move.

"Are you okay?" I probe.

"Me? Yeah."

I let the silence fester.

"Okay. I…I've been burdened by yesterday. Not the news about kidnapping…I mean…don't get me wrong. I'm worried about that. But the discussion of danger…It opened old wounds. Reminded me of stuff that really bothered me. Things you said about death."

"Things I said about death?" I'm perplexed.

"Well...what you said about life-after-death. About getting to heaven."

Her comment surprises me. Shocks me actually. I wasn't expecting that. But I'm good at hiding my emotions, staying neutral. "Hmm...What do you mean? Tell me more."

She takes a deep breath. "You remember talking to my Mom about God, when she was sick? About Jesus being the Savior for our sins? The way...the only way to heaven?"

"Yeah," I nod, as we continue to stroll along the road.

"I'm glad for my mom. I do believe heaven is real and...she's there." She smiles, seemingly comforted at the thought. However, I sense an obvious "but" coming.

"But I really struggle with this 'Jesus is the only way' idea," she says with air quotes. Then she holds her hands up, in a surrender fashion. "Don't get me wrong, I respect you Lucy – I do. And I'm happy for my mom. But I have to be honest – this really bothered me. More than you know. To think Christianity is the only way? That's kinda...arrogant...I think it's disrespectful to other people." She finishes with a sheepish tone, as if concerned she's insulting me, by saying I'm being disrespectful.

Years ago, I would have fired back. I. would have snapped at the suggestion of my being arrogant. But I've learned that sharing spiritual truth is about winning a person, not an argument. I've learned that taking a different approach is more effective – using questions to get someone to reflect on their position and consider why Christianity makes sense.[37]

"Honestly, Tabitha, I'm glad you told me. I felt like something was bothering you but didn't know what it was. Trust me when I say I'm not bothered at all. And...and I understand what you're saying. I used to think that way a long time ago."

"I didn't know if I would insult you by sharing how I felt," she says.

"Not all. Really," I assure her.

"I know we have other things to worry about right now, like

survival and defending our community," she admits. "But this new threat is compelling me to reconsider life-after-death."

I decide to stop talking. Do I say anything else? Does Tabitha want me to respond further? Or did she just want to vent emotion? I get my answer immediately.

"So, you see what I'm saying," Tabitha says. "You agree…it's kinda of disrespectful. Unloving."

"I don't agree," I answer matter-of-factly, but in a friendly manner. "Actually, I think one of the most loving things you can do is disagree with someone respectfully and share truth. Especially something as important as the truth about God and our eternal destination. Can I share my reasons why I believe Christianity is the only way?"

"Of course," she seems sincere, maybe relieved I would say that.

"Let me ask a few questions," I say, as we continue to stroll along. "First, do you think this idea of only one way to heaven, is my idea or a claim from Jesus?"

"Yeah, I understand. You would say it's from Jesus." She smiles at me. "I remember the things you told my mom…um…that Jesus said He is the way, the truth and the life, and no one comes to the Father except by Him.[38]"

"Good memory," I'm genuinely impressed.

"It's not a compliment," Tabitha frowns "I remember it because it bothered me. It was stuck in my mind, like a bad song I couldn't get out of my head."

"I hear you. But you see my point, that it's not my idea. It was Jesus who claimed He is the only way to heaven. Since Jesus claimed to be God, and proved it, we should take seriously what He says about spiritual truth. Here's my second question. Is it possible for two ideas that contradict to both be true?"

Tabitha pauses. I think the answer is obvious, but maybe she's trying to think of an example.

"I'm not sure. I guess not," she says.

"It's not a trick," I say. "Two ideas that contradict cannot both be true at the same time, and in the same sense.[39] For example,

Christians say Jesus died on a cross and Muslims say Jesus did not die on a cross. Either one could be right, but both cannot be true, correct?"

"Sure. I agree with that," she concedes.

"That's why I told your Mom it's not possible for all religions to be true. They have fundamental beliefs that contradict, so they cannot all be true. They cannot all be genuine ways to go to heaven. Therefore, it would be unloving to agree with this belief."

"Hmmm...I guess so." She seems to be thinking through it; maybe trying to find a flaw in my reasoning. However, it's not my opinion, but rather a fundamental law of logic.

"Why didn't I understand that before?" she says, seemingly wondering out loud.

"Before D6 changed the world, our society was conditioned to believe all truth is relative, the idea that each person could have their own truth; and it was intolerant or wrong to say otherwise. All of that was a lie."

"Really?" Tabitha says, as if stunned by the insight.

"Yeah. Most people fell for it – me included."

"Honestly, my head is spinning."

"The main point is each person cannot have their own truth about God. It might sound nice to say each person can have their own truth, but it's not possible. Creating and worshiping your own god, that fits your desires, is idolatry." I pause a couple seconds to let that point sink in; then I continue. "Last question. Is it loving to affirm a belief that someone has if you know it's false?"

"Well, if I was married and got fat, I wouldn't want my husband to tell me that," she giggles.

I chuckle too. "Well, you're not fat, and with our food supply I don't think either of us will be overweight any time soon." We have a light-hearted laugh.

"But this is not about being polite," I say. "I'm talking about important matters, such as health and safety. Is it loving to affirm someone's belief if you're convinced it's false? If you're reasonably sure they are making a decision that would lead to harm, is it loving to affirm the false path they are on?"

"No. Definitely not." Tabitha's voice tails off, as if realizing the admission.

I decide not to say anything further; just let my points resonate with her, hopefully. We continue our trek on the cold day. My cheeks feel numb.

After a few minutes, she finally breaks the silence, "So I understand your point. It makes sense, but it still makes me uneasy... telling people they're wrong."

"But if you share your view in a gentle and respectful way, isn't that better than affirming something that is false and could lead to serious danger? And if you don't say anything, isn't that basically giving them a false sense of security for the danger they are headed for?"

"Only if it's true."

"That's fair. The key question to consider is this: Is the truth about God something we decide or discover? In other words, is it based on our personal opinion or a reality independent of our preferences?"

"I guess we discover it, but what's wrong with just letting people believe what they want?" she asks.

"Because if someone is wrong, they don't simply lose their life, they are punished for eternity."

"You have an answer everything," Tabitha says with a smile.

I let out a loud laugh. "Definitely not. But I'm really glad you brought it up. You know I don't think there's anything more important."

As friends before her Mom passed away, I talked to her multiple times about God. But she just listened. She didn't question or counter. This was the first time she started to engage a bit.

The distant howl of a wolf interrupts our conversation. I've learned not to disregard the sounds of animals. More than once, I assumed I was at a safe distance, only to have a predator get uncomfortably close. One time I heard a faint growl to the side of me while I was checking a trap. I mistakenly thought it was farther away than it was, and a fisher cat viciously approached me. Fortunately, I had a spear in hand and fended it off before it could reach me. As it retreated, I noticed younglings it was protecting.

I assume we are done talking until Tabitha interrupts the silence.

"But we should respect what people believe about themselves, right? I mean, let's say I agree that the truth about God is not based on opinion; but if someone believes something about themselves, we should accept it as true, right?"

I wonder if Tabitha's question may relate to herself. Does she believe something about herself I might not agree with?

"I don't agree that is true in all cases," I say, shaking my head back-and-forth. "Honestly, I don't mean to be such a contrarian; but there are many times people believe something about themselves and it's not true."

"Like what?" she says, challenging my position.

I have several personal examples I could share. Lies that I let myself believe when I was younger that attacked my self-worth, which now I know are false. Instead, I try to recall examples I had read in Dad's notebook.

"What if someone believes they are a loser with no value?" I ask. "Is that accurate? Is it true just because they believe it? I don't think that is true at all; and that is certainly not what the Bible says. All people are made in the image of God, so they have intrinsic value. Everyone is of tremendous worth. Everyone. And that cannot be taken from them. A lot of what we believe about human beings and the world around us is based on the truth about God; it provides the foundation for reality."

"Well, I agree with that people aren't losers. We're all different though."

"Yeah. We all have different personalities, emotions we feel, things we like, et cetera. But we don't decide foundational truths about ourselves as human beings. Those come from our Creator."

I glance at Tabitha and see a mix of expressions. She seems more relaxed, perhaps relieved to have gotten a burden off her shoulders. But her wrinkled forehead indicates she is still thinking through it.

I didn't expect such a deep conversation this morning. I was just hoping to chat as friends which we haven't done in such a long time. Nonetheless, the conversation has helped me forget the cold and pass the time. She asks a few more innocuous questions, and we continue our friendly discussion.

Finally, I see the wide river come into view and realize we are getting close to the marina. As we scale a small hill, the area opens up and the river comes fully into view.

Tabitha points. "There it is. The marina."

I stop to take in the scene. There are a couple smaller boats as well as the two large catamarans we came to inspect. There's a one-story building on the edge of the river that a long time ago sold food and supplies and provided restrooms. A large parking lot with pockets of broken asphalt is in front of the structure. Tall grass has emerged from holes in the tar; and there are a few rusted cars, stranded for many years.

To the right of the building is an open area with a concrete walking path along the river that runs under a bridge; and the left side has twenty acres of woods with trails. When I was a kid, I used to walk those trails with my parents. What was once beautiful scenery along the river, is now probably home to dangerous predators.

I scan the area for signs of danger. Nothing. At least nothing visible.

"Ready?" Tabitha asks.

"Yeah."

We proceed cautiously toward the marina. My senses are heighted. I'm attentive, looking for danger. I hold my shotgun tight. My anxiety builds as we traverse the parking lot. Tabitha doesn't seem to be nervous; rather simply making her way to the boat. Me? I'm constantly considering potential danger. Is there something hiding behind this tall grass? No. I need to walk to the right a few steps so I can see behind one of the cars. Again, no threat.

As we get closer to the building, I see much of the glass is shattered and part of the roof is caving in. There are large cracks in the walls. It looks as though the structure could collapse at any moment. Anyway, no need to enter it. I'm sure there's nothing of value, and we could be walking into the home of an animal, maybe one protecting its young. We proceed around the right of the building.

I'm still searching intently for danger, but it's a relatively quiet morning. There is some wind, though; and it's blowing in the direction toward the woods to our left. I don't like it. It could be carrying our scent to large carnivores. That's the way my mind works now. Always considering worse-case scenarios. It's helped me survive.

We are closer to the docks now and I have a better look at the two catamarans. They're still afloat. That's a good start.

There are five docks at this marina, and the two catamarans are farthest away, closest to the wooded area. Being the biggest boats, they have a separate dock to themselves.

There are a few sailboats that are sunken, showing their mast sticking out of the water at an angle. Several smaller boats are still afloat, connected to docks; but most don't look to be in good shape. Maybe one of them could be used. The winter weather has clearly taken a toll on them. From a distance, the catamarans appear to be in much better shape.

As we approach the large sailboats, the effects of weather on the aesthetics becomes apparent. Paint is peeling from years of sun, precipitation and changing temperatures. Areas of canvas are faded from UV rays. But these are cosmetics that I could care less about.

Tabitha steps onto the dock and heads toward the catamarans that are about fifteen feet from the riverbank. I stop and turn around, surveying the area again, checking for any signs of life, not only for animals, but also humans. I wouldn't expect the latter, but you never know.

It remains eerily silent, but I shouldn't be surprised by that. This time of the year, with some animals approaching hibernation, it gets particularly quiet. Other than Tabitha's footsteps on the wooden dock, I don't hear anything. I don't see any movement anywhere. I decide all is well and follow Tabitha's path along the dock.

The two boats are across from each other, on either side of the wooden dock.

"Hello?" Tabitha calls out. "Anyone here?"

There's no response.

With a pistol in hand, Tabitha enters the boat to the right, stepping onto the transom in the rear. I follow her lead and am relieved it's solid. I was worried it may be rotting, but it feels sturdy.

There is an entrance to the level underneath. Tabitha pokes her head inside and looks around, while I continue to scan the outside. I notice a couple small animal droppings on the floor, maybe the size of a small rodent, but they are clearly not fresh.

"I'm going to look around," Tabitha says. I decide it's best to follow her, in case something, anything, is waiting in ambush. I see Tabitha grip the handgun with both hands. She swings the barrel back-and-forth as she scans the first room inside. It's a comfortable place to relax just inside the boat with a small table and sofas. I can see to the right and left, that there are a few steps leading down. I recall checking the two bedrooms on either side for supplies a long time ago.

Tabitha goes left and checks the area leading to the bedrooms of this side of the boat.

"See anything?" I ask

"Nothing."

I continue to follow her, guarding against a surprise and listening for anything that could be coming up behind us.

It's uneventful. One bedroom seems to have been left untouched, while the other is mattress only; no blankets. We go to the other side, and the results are the same. I expected worse. Damage or a mess. But obviously nobody considered there to be anything of value.

We immediately go to the second boat. This time I take lead. The conclusion is the same as our first search. But for whatever reason, this one has been entirely stripped of supplies and blankets. Only the furniture and mattresses remain. It doesn't matter. The condition is better than I expected. There's no water on the floors indicating leaks. No animals that have taken residence. The structure seems fine.

We decide it's time for a rest and some food. We've been going for a couple hours now and I'm feeling the pains of hunger. We rest in one of the bedrooms of the second boat and fill our stomachs with the food we brought and much needed water. Our discussion is light, mainly reminiscing about previous events we shared together. It feels like our friendship is being rekindled.

After resting for some time, we decide it's time to head home. As I pack my bag, I'm startled by the sudden sound of wild animals fighting outside, toward land. I dash to a window in the bedroom and see a pack of wolves attacking something large on the ground.

"What is it?" Tabitha asks, joining my side to examine the scene.

"I don't know. Maybe a deer."

"Four. Five. Maybe six wolves," she counts.

The savage feast is only ten feet from the wooden dock for these catamarans. I consider some alternatives and settle on a strategy. I grip my shotgun as I consider I will need to fire a shot and scare the wolves away, long enough to allow us to escape from being trapped on the dock. Then we can head home as they resume eating.

"What are you thinking?" Tabitha asks.

As I explain the plan, her expression gradually transitions from a grimace to disapproval. "What if they turn on us? You know, protecting their food."

"I think if we move quickly, they'll leave us alone and just return to their meal."

"You *think*?" she obviously didn't like my word choice, but obviously I can't guarantee it.

"Why don't we wait a while until they finish eating?" Tabitha proposes. "We're putting ourselves in danger."

"But they could hang around and feed on the carcass for days," I respond.

"At least let them get full before we try to get by them."

"Maybe. Let's get in better position to check it out."

I move to the door of this fourth bedroom and peak out. Nothing. I point the shotgun to the lounge area and let out a breath I didn't realize I was holding.

I step into the small hallway and quietly creep up the steps leading into the living space, listening for any signs of danger. Slowly, I take steps, one-by-one, straining to hear the wolves.

Suddenly multiple growls and barks erupt from the wolves outside. Are they fighting each other?

"What's happening?" Tabitha whispers from behind me.

"I don't know."

Then I hear a massive roar. Was that a bear? Barking from the wolves intensities. There is heavy commotion, as if a massive battle is taking place. This went from bad to worse.

I move to the back of the boat, so I can see outside, A massive grizzly bear is next to the carcass, growling and swinging at wolves.

I step back inside the lounge area. I look at Tabitha who looks distressed. I'm sure she's terrified of the wolves, given what happened to her mom. I remember that feeling when I was flying fifteen years ago through a terrible storm that ended in a crash. I was paralyzed with fear. Adding a grizzly significantly elevates the danger.

"We'll stay here," I reassure her. "Let things come down."

Tabitha nods nervously.

After a few seconds, the vicious fighting noises outside have quieted slightly. I wonder if I should stay hidden, but my curiosity wins out and I decide to peek again. But just as I stick my head out, I'm startled by a wolf, running down the dock, apparently fleeing the area.

Does it see me? I think so. Where is it headed?

I raise my gun to fire. It seems to be heading for me. I'm surprised at its aggressiveness.

I fire a shot, that sends me off balance. The scatter seems to have hit it the wolf, but it doesn't stop. Now within range, it jumps before I can fire a second shot, attacking my torso. It's all I can do to stick the middle part of my gun barrel in its mouth. The force of its attack sends me on my back inside the boat, with the wolf on top of me. I see its fangs clenched around the barrel.

A sudden memory of horror surfaces; a long time ago, when I was attacked by a dog that bit my arm. The terrible event clearly left an emotional scar that just reemerged.

One of the wolf's paws presses on my left shoulder, pinning me against the floor. Its teeth unclench from the barrel and snap at my head. I smack its snout with the barrel to keep it from biting my flesh. It snaps again, lunging at my face. I dodge my head to the side and hear the snap of teeth inches from my skin.

I'm going to get bit. It feels inevitable. If I try to roll, I'll expose myself. I need to stay focused on defense. But it feels like it will get me.

Bang!

The sound of a gunshot startles me; the wolf is sent flying off me toward the back of the boat. It yelps and rolls. I look and see it falling off the side of the boat. I turn back and see Tabitha with her gun aimed in my direction.

"Lucy? Are you alright? I'm sorry. It happened so fast!"

"I'm okay," I assure her.

As I pull myself to my feet, I see another wolf running down the wooden dock, about to reach the boat. I don't know if it has the same aggressive intentions, but I assume the worst.

"Tabitha!" I yell.

She sees it and fires, but misses.

I aim my shotgun and fire just as it is approaching the boat. It collapses instantly. Tabitha fires again, but the animal is not moving from its prone position on the dock. I killed it.

We both step out from inside the boat to observe the scene. A massive grizzly bear is growling and swiping at a wolf, maybe twenty-five feet from us. The wolf springs backward to avoid the attack. Another wolf is several feet to the side of the engagement and two other wolves have clearly retreated from the action. The bear has clearly taken control of the carcass. I look to the right and notice two small cubs keeping its distance from the engagement.

My heart sinks. The scene has just gotten incredibly more dangerous.

"Tabitha, look!" I say pointing at the cubs "See them?"

"I do." Her voice is nervous.

The mother bear charges the closest wolf, which quickly retreats.

The wolves clearly give up their meal to the bears. A long time ago, I thought bears only ate berries and nuts, but now I know they are omnivores, eating both plants and animals.

"They're probably preparing for hibernation," Tabitha says softly.

"Mother bear," I mutter. "No way we can slip by them. No way. She will defend them ferociously."

Tabitha looks up at the sky. "We only have so much daylight. If they stay for a while, we won't get home."

I notice the large bear stand upright on its hind legs. It looks to be about nine feet tall. Its cubs wander over to the corpse. Mother bear looks in our direction. I wonder if she can smell us.

"We should get back inside," I say. "Even though we're a good distance away, she may get spooked . She's going to be highly protective."

We step backward, retreating into the lounge area. I turn and head to the first bedroom on the right, back to the one from where we first saw the action, positioning ourselves so we can see the land. Tabitha follows and closes the door. My mind is swirling, analyzing our options.

"What if they don't leave Lucy? I mean, until it gets dark?"

"I don't know. I'm worried about not being home to protect my son from potential abductors, but we have to be smart."

"I agree. I mean, honestly, I don't…I can't travel in the dark. The wolves…" She just shakes her head, and I'm sure she is thinking about her mom.

"I hear you," I say, looking outside, hoping the scene has changed. It hasn't. The bears cubs are feeding, while Mom keeps guard. "We'll make a prudent decision," I assure her.

Seconds turn into minutes and then to hours; eventually, sunlight begins to retreat. The situation isn't changing, not enough to journey home tonight. The reality of not being home to watch over Zach, with this risk of abduction, is terrifying me. And from this distance, I cannot communicate with Peter by radio. The morning cannot come soon enough.

The room has one bed and a few comfortable chairs. I insist

Jason M. Jolin

Tabitha take the bed. I prefer the chair so that I can stay by the window to monitor activity outside, even though the lack of light makes it challenging.

My concerns have been steadily rising, much worse than an hour ago. As darkness increases, so do my fears. My anxiety is always worse at night. I decide there is nothing left to do except pray.

CHAPTER
THIRTEEN

I see movement flash across the floor, which is only faintly illuminated. Whatever it was, it was small, but inside the room. It's the middle of the night. The room is dark. Pale light from the moon provides only a hint of visibility.

My mind begins to process what it saw. There was movement – in the room! Something small, but a live animal. Danger!

I click my flashlight on, and see multiple small creatures scurry away to cover. Rats? I think they're rats! I shine the light over at the bed, but it's empty. Where is Tabitha? Why did she leave the room without telling me? Did she get bit?

I stand up from the chair and check behind me. Nothing. I fervently scan the room with my light, looking for movement.

Suddenly a rodent dashes from under the bed, racing toward me. It's clearly attacking. When it gets within a few inches, I kick it away with my right sneaker. I flash the light around the room and see another rat emerge, scurrying toward me. I try to kick it with my left foot, but the rat attaches itself to my sneaker. I shake my foot to disconnect it, but it hangs on in mid-air. I kick my foot against the bed to detach it.

A third and fourth rat emerges. The room is infested! I need to escape! I hurry to the door, open and slam it shut. The hallway is dark, but I can see the steps leading to the lounge area. I have my flashlight but no gun to defend myself; and no armor on my forearms or shins. I need to find Tabitha and then somehow get our gear. I proceed to the steps and look around the lounge before entering. Similar to the bedroom, it's faintly lit from celestial light.

"Tabitha?" I call. "Where are you?"

I hear growling from the darkness to my right. It's coming from the other bedroom on this side of the boat. Without seeing it, I know it is the snarling of a wolf. I can't tell how close it is, but it was loud enough for me know the door is open. I feel exposed. My fear is increasing rapidly. Do I try to get to the bedroom door and close it before being attacked, or make a break for it? Immediately, I decide to race for the dock, get to the other boat and barricade behind closed doors.

As I begin to run, I hear the panting wolf sprinting toward me. I scamper through the dark. But as I reach outside and jump onto the wooden dock, I run right into the space of the large grizzly bear, the one that was feeding on the carcass yesterday. It roars ferociously and swipes at me. I throw myself backward to avoid the attack and fall on my back on the dock.

My legs are vulnerable to attack from the bear. I consider scrambling backward, but the wolf that was chasing me is instantly at my head. Its legs are at my shoulders. I feel the fur of one leg against my neck. The bear comes into view at my feet. Its menacing growl reveals its sharp teeth. I'm surrounded and completely vulnerable. I want to move; punch the wolf's snout before it attacks, roll and scramble to my feet to run to safety, but I can't move. I'm paralyzed with fear.

I consider rolling off the dock into the water, but I feel the wolf pull at my shirt with its teeth, as if trying to protect its meal. Me. I'm about to bitten; yanked from both ends. I'm like the carcass the bear and wolves previously battled over. I need to get out of here.

I punch the wolf's nose with my right hand to release its grips; but before I can pull my hand away, the wolf bites it. I feel its sharp teeth around my palm. I'm bit! I'm bit!

I'm jolted into consciousness, gasping for air. It's dark. My left hand grabs the arm of the chair I'm sitting on, while I try to comprehend where I am. My right hand grabs a flashlight and scans the room, looking for predators. There's no wolf. No bear. No rats. I switch the flashlight to my left hand and check my right palm – no bite marks. Tabitha is sleeping in bed. It takes me a moment to understand what happened. It was a dream. A nightmare.

Night terrors about animals attacking are common for everyone in this new world. Almost everyone has them, and they're terrifying. I hadn't had one in several weeks; and this one felt especially real. Obviously, the scene yesterday was the catalyst for my nightmare.

I place my right hand over my rapidly beating heart. I feel heavy thumping. I take several deep breaths to settle my nerves. After a few minutes, I pull myself out of the chair and look outside. Hints of sunlight are beginning to brighten the outdoors.

With the flashlight still in hand, I pick up my shotgun and quietly make my way to the door of the room. I listen for movement, snarling, breathing, any signs of an animal on the other side of the door. Nothing.

I open and peak into the hall, scanning for danger. I flash the light into the dark space. All seems clear. I step out of the room and close the door, continuing to listen for signs of peril. Still nothing.

I press the shotgun against my right shoulder, hold the barrel and flashlight pointed ahead with my left hand and keep my right finger on the trigger. As I proceed toward the lounge area, I notice the door to the other bedroom is open. I remind myself the snarling wolf was a dream. I shine the light anyway just to check. Again, nothing.

I decide to proceed to the back of the boat and outside. The barrel of the gun follows my search. I keep my finger on the trigger of the shotgun ready to shoot; but there continues to be no signs of danger. The sun has risen enough to illuminate the area, albeit faintly. I click the flashlight off and place it in my back pocket.

I survey the scene on land, checking to see if the bear and cubs are still present. I immediately see the dead wolf I shot, still lying on the dock. Then I see two wolves feeding on the carcass, but no sign of the bears. A couple other wolves are a short distance away. My guess is the bears had their fill last night and vacated the area; and the wolves then came back to fill their stomachs. I presume they have been feeding for some time for two of them not to be eating.

I hear the door open. "Lucy?"

"Out here."

I continue to observe the wolves as Tabitha makes her way over to me.

"The bears are gone," I whisper.

"Good. The wolves?"

"They're back," I say, pointing toward them.

"Hmmm," Tabitha mutters, as she squints. "You want to push through them, don't you?" she asks with a hint of trepidation.

I know she has an aversion to wolves but I'm eager to get home. "I think we can scare them off with a gunshot."

Tabitha sighs heavily. "Still only four of them?"

"Yeah. We'll be careful," I say confidently. "I'll take lead."

Neither of us are interested in eating. Tabitha fears the wolves and I'm anxious to see Zach. We gather our supplies and exit the boat. Only one wolf is continuing to eat, the largest of the pack. The others are standing close by. I wonder if they will be less aggressive since they've already eaten.

As we proceed slowly down the dock, I watch for any indication whether they will retreat or attack. The carcass is a short way from the end of the dock. I keep the butt of the reloaded shotgun tight to my shoulder. I'm still wondering whether we can slip by them or need to fire a shot to scare them away. Maybe firing at them would trigger an attack. I don't think so, but who knows.

I remind myself to be careful. We're approaching danger. Focus. Getting bit now would almost certainly be fatal.

As we reach the end of the dock, I slow my pace. The wolf closest to us is still feeding on the carcass. But as I get closer it, it stops tearing off pieces of meat. Its eyes glare into mine, a scowl that is sinister. As I step off the deck, onto the pavement, the wolf shows its teeth. Its menacing snarl is intimidating.

But I can't show fear. Stepping back is not an option. If we retreat, who knows what other predators may visit the carcass. I won't back down from this challenge.

I feel my arms beginning to tremble, trying to keep the heavy gun steady, while the rest of my body shakes with fear. It's one thing to react to danger; it's quite different to intentionally approach it. I grip the shotgun even tighter, maintaining my aim at the wolf. It opens its mouth, revealing its fangs. Animal flesh hangs out the side of its mouth.

"Lucy?" Tabitha says softly with panic.

I don't answer. This is not the time to talk, or retreat. The wolf steps forward and I don't hesitate. I squeeze the trigger of the shotgun. The shot thunders loudly. The wolf yelps and staggers backward. It limps away, alive, but wounded. The other wolves retreat, following the direction of its injured pack member.

I exhale loudly, and drop my head, relieved danger is no longer within range. But moments later I shake the thought – I need to get home. "Let's go Tabitha."

As we begin walking, I pop open the shotgun and remove the used shell. I replace it and snap the gun closed. We don't chit chat; we just move.

After about thirty minutes of walking, we're almost half-way home. I am startled by a voice coming over the radio. I had turned it on, but I didn't think I was in range yet. It sounds like Peter, in-between heavy static. His tone is panicked. "Gus? ...med? Are... there? I...help...is missing."

My eyes grow wide. Missing? Someone is missing? My stomach explodes with butterflies.

"Peter!" I scream into the radio.

Static crackles as Peter replies. "...goodness your alive. Where...you?"

"Peter? I can't understand you."

"Lucy?...you there?"

"Peter? Who is missing?"

"...home. Zach...missing."

A jolt of terror strikes by body like a bolt of lightning, like nothing I have ever felt before. Immediately, I throw my backpack off my shoulders and begin to sprint for home.

"Lucy. I'm coming," Tabitha calls from behind.

Part of me wants to drop my shotgun so I can pump my arms harder, run faster, but that would be foolish. Obviously, I may need it.

I'm running down the main street that connects to my road. I search for a van while I run. I dread the thought, but if someone has abducted Zach, I need to intercept the vehicle.

As I rush home, staticky words come over the radio in my left hand. I click the button and yell into it. "Whoever can hear me. It's Lucy. I'm coming home!" After less than two minutes, I already feel my lungs burning, I don't think I can keep up this pace, but fear propels me.

"...cy?" It's Peter voice. "Are you there?"

"Peter. I'm here!" I yell into the radio as I continue to press forward.

"Lucy. You're breaking..."

My lungs are on fire. I just keep running, trying to close the gap to eliminate the static.

"Lucy?!"

"Peter. I'm coming!" I shout, still looking for moving vehicles. "Where is Zach?"

"He's missing. I don't think he was abducted. But I can't find him in the woods. I'm sorry!"

I don't know what this means, but Zach is missing. I'm relieved he wasn't taken, but the thought of him being lost in the woods. Could he have been bitten? If I find him, will I watch him being tortured to death by D63? I can't...I won't consider it. I block the thought.

I round the corner and head down my street, running as fast as I can. My pace has slowed, but adrenaline is driving me forward.

I see Gus and Ahmed farther down the road, hurrying toward my house.

"Peter! Where are you?" I yell into the radio.

"I'm in back of our house. About a hundred yards."

"Were coming!" Ahmed screams into the radio.

I can't traverse my street fast enough. Panic bombards my sanity. Will I ever see my son again? Is he in pain?

"Peter. I'm coming!" I cannot wait to get an explanation. "What happened?" I'm gasping for breath.

"Lucy. I'm sorry…" Peter is out of breath.

"What happened?" I shout.

"We were checking small traps when a mountain lion appeared. It blocked our path from getting home. We retreated up the mountain."

I know what Peter means by 'mountain.' It's not really a mountain, but a large hill, maybe forty feet high, with numerous jagged rocks, crevices, and small caves.

"We headed for the top. When the mountain lion pursued us, I stopped to shoot it with my rifle…But my shot missed and I lost my balance, tumbling down the hill. When I stopped, I fired again at the mountain lion, but it ran off after Zach." Peter's tone is anguish. "Zach ran over the hill to the other side. It took me time to reach the top. I was dizzy…When I got there…I couldn't find him. I called for him, but he was nowhere. I'm sorry!" At this point, Peter is weeping.

Tears are streaming down my cheeks. *My son!*

Eventually I reach my house and run directly into the backyard. A part of me wants to collapse from exhaustion, but I won't. I can't give up. *Please God,* I pray. *Please be with Zach. Please help us.*

Finally, I see Peter. He's at the base of the mountain. Gus and Ahmed are with him, bent over, gasping for breath. As I close the distance, I see Peter's head is wounded. He looks at me with agony.

"I'm sorry," he says again.

Part of me wants to scream at him. *You had one main job while I was gone – protect Zach!* But I don't have time. My focus is finding my son.

"Zaaaaach!" I scream. No response. "Where was he last?" I can barely say the words. I'm drained from running for so long. I feel the need to vomit, but I refuse.

Peter points up the hill. "He was toward the top. He may have run down and hid in the forest. I looked but didn't see him. I came back for help."

The image of a mountain lion pops into my mind; and I get a pit in my stomach. The thought of Zach being attacked pushes me forward. I don't wait for further explanation. I begin to jog up the mountain. At this point, I'm not capable of running. From the crunch of stones behind me I know others are following.

As I proceed, I scan the large, jagged rocks I am passing; they create big crevices that could easily hide a mountain lion.

"How big is it?" I ask Peter, trying to determine what cracks could conceal the dangerous predator. Ironically, I'm hoping to run into it, rather than have it pursuing or attacking my son.

"Big..." he pants. "Really big." That's disturbing, but I can't get more frightened.

We continue to jog up the gradual slope, taking turns calling for Zach. We're also checking between rocks and behind boulders. Within minutes we're at the top of the hill. I scan the descending slope. There are a few trees, but it's filled with rocks and crevices. At the bottom is the beginning of a large forest that carries on for several hundred yards before reaching the real mountains, much larger than the hill I stand on.

"Zaaaaach!" I yell again; but hear nothing except the heavy breaths of my companions. I see no movement among the leaves. The thought of him being ambushed by the deadly mountain lion enters my mind. I visualize him crying out for help, calling for me...I expel the terrible thought from my mind. I can't consider the horror of my son being taken from me by a vicious animal.

"Zaaaaach!" I shout with all my might. Nothing.

I look at Peter. He has a terrified look on his face. I'm not giving up. I begin to descend the mountain with urgency, not being careful about my progress. I don't care if I'm attacked if my son is gone. I'm heading for the forest. My hope is Zach ran as fast as he could, and now is out of ear shot.

We get to the bottom of the hill.

"Zaaaaach!" Peter screams. We all scan the thick forest ahead of us. I listen for even the faintest response. A cry for help. Anything. I feel helpless. I'm desperate for something. I can't stop. Thinking about possibilities right now will destroy me.

I'm the first to step into the forest. I could be stepping into danger. A snake. A fisher cat. I don't care. Avoiding danger is not my primary concern. We progress several feet into the forest when I think I hear something.

"Stop!" I yell to everyone. "Quiet!"

"Help." I hear a faint voice from a child.

"Zaaaach!" I yell.

"Mommm!"

It's Zach! He's alive! It sounds like he's back at the hill.

"I'm coming!" I hurry out of the forest. Is he injured? Is he dying? We get to the base of the hill.

"Zaaaach!" Peter shouts. "Where are you?"

"Help," Zach calls weakly.

I sprint toward the location, which seems to be halfway up the hill. I don't see anything. Where is he?

"Help," Zach calls again. I get to the spot where his voice is coming from, but I don't see him.

"Zach!" I call.

"Mom." Again his voice is weak. He's inside the rocks. I begin to scan the crevices. Peter, Gus and Ahmed do the same.

I see him! He is maybe eight feet down, between a narrow crack. He looks wedged in tight.

"Zach!" I call. I'm so relieved he is alive. "Are you okay?"

"Mom. Please. I'm stuck." He's panicking. His eyes meet mine. They divulge his fear.

I look for a way to get down to him, but the sides of the rock are steep and smooth. I would simply slide down and not be able to get back up. I look around for something to lower down to him.

"Lucy. Use this." Ahmed had the same idea. He gives me a solid stick about four feet long.

"Peter get my feet." I throw myself into the crevice and extend the stick to him.

"Zach. Reach for it," I demand. His arms look stuck. "Push Zach. You got this."

His expression changes from distress to determination. He pushes his arms forward, enough to grab the stick.

"Hold tight," I order. I try to pull the stick toward me, but he doesn't move. *Please God.* I try to yank again, but I have little leverage. *Please God.* I try a third time, with all my might, screaming with determination. He moves several inches.

"Hold tight," I say. Reaching further down on the stick, I pull hard and get him closer. I repeat this until he is within reach. I grab his small hands, so thankful to be able to touch my son again, this side of heaven.

"I have you," I pull him to my shoulders. "Peter, pull us up."

My brother lifts us from the crevice. As we emerge from the crack, I hold his face between my hands and look into his eyes, "Are you okay? Are you hurt?"

"My head hurts." I see a large bump on the side of his head. "I tried to run. I fell, I think. I don't remember."

He must have stumbled when he tried to flee the mountain lion and fell into this crevice. Probably banged his head and went unconscious.

I touch his arms and legs to make sure nothing is broken; he seems to be okay. *Thank you God!*

"We should get home," Peter says. "The mountain lion could still be around."

We make it home without encountering the mountain lion. We have a hot meal, while Peter and I share our encounters. I discuss the catamarans as a way to flee the area, if necessary. I can tell they're exhausted because it's barely dark before they both decide they want sleep.

After kissing Zach goodnight, I feel compelled to check the locks on the doors – again. Front door first. Deadbolt and chain lock? Check. I take a heavy-duty security bar and brace it under the door handle. Is it adequate against a potential intruder? I hope so. Am I going to sleep tonight? Maybe, but it certainly won't be restful. And

I probably won't rest well any time soon; until I know abduction is not a threat.

I check the rear door. Triple locked – deadbolt, chain and latch. Windows are nailed shut. The basement door, which opens by swinging inside, has two 2x4s across the door held in place by metal brackets. There's nothing left to do, but I'm still nervous.

I ascend to the 2nd floor. Peter and Zach are sleeping in the same room; Peter in bed and Zach on the floor tucked away in a sleeping bag. I head over to the corner bedroom in the front of the house that is on the street and closest to our home. It gives me the best view for surveillance of our house.

I take my rifle in hand and sit on the folding chair I positioned at a side window. The night has a haze to it, making visibility a little challenging. I place the weapon against my shoulder and look through the scope. I have a good view of the area at the front door of my home. Now, let's just hope that if an intruder comes, that's the house they attack, not the one we are in.

CHAPTER
FOURTEEN

I'm startled awake by a voice shouting through the handheld radio next to me. It's dark; middle of the night is my guess. I'm a mix of panic and groggy, not fully awake or aware of what is happening. I didn't comprehend the words that woke me.

"Is anyone there?" Ahmed says through the radio. "I see a vehicle!" I recall it was his turn to take watch in the house we call *The Tower*. "Is anyone there?" Ahmed's voice is filled with nervousness.

This is the first time there has been an interruption at night. It's been two weeks since Tabitha and I visited the catamarans. I was starting to think, and hope, abductors would never come.

I grab the radio. "Ahmed. It's Lucy. I'm here. What do you see?"

"Lucy! Thank goodness," he sounds out-of-breath. "I saw headlights far down the road. A vehicle coming this way. I'm sure of it. But the lights went off. It's dark, but it looks like a van...maybe... it stopped at the trees we cut down to block the road."

As Ahmed has been talking, I've put on jeans and grabbed a sweatshirt. I take the handgun on my nightstand and tuck it in the back of my jeans.

"Peter!" I yell. "Are you awake?"

Nothing. He sleeps like a rock but come on!

"I see people!" Ahmed says anxiously. "Two figures have exited the vehicle. They're jogging this way!"

My eyes grow wide. This is happening. We're being invaded.

"Code one," Ahmed says into the radio. It's the words we chose to alert everyone that intruders have entered our community, and all should hide. "Whoever can hear me, I repeat, code one."

"Keep watching," I respond.

Leo, Dario, and Sophia check in by radio. Ahmed tells them to stay hidden; and he'll let them know if they head in their direction, which is one street over from us.

I exit the bedroom and open the door to where Peter and Zach are sleeping. "Peter! Get up!" I yell.

He jumps out of bed, clearly disheveled. What? What is it?"

"Abductors are here. Stay with Zach."

"Mom?" Zach says nervously.

"Stay with Uncle Peter. No matter what."

I don't wait for a response. I run down the hall and quickly descend to the first floor. I'm not exactly sure what I'm going to do yet. It's one thing to prepare for a crisis; but it's different when it actually happens, and stress is soaring. I'm sticking with the plan; grab a rifle and wait at the front door to see if I need to hide or fight. I have never had to shoot at a person, but I'm prepared to, if necessary to defend my family and community.

"They've reached Gus's house," Ahmed says, his voice a bit quieter.

I hope they fall for the trap. We attached a contraption to the front door that pulls a string tied to a flash grenade. A few seconds after the pin is pulled, the grenade will explode with a blinding flash of light, intended to stun and disorient the intruders.

At that point, we've decided to use caution engaging the abductors. If they collapse without a weapon, we could approach with guns drawn to capture and question them. If they begin randomly shooting, we could stay hidden or attempt to take them down. Otherwise, we could simply let them leave. Whether the scheme enables us to capture them or not, they will know this community will defend itself.

"They are walking past house one," Ahmed says with a nervous tone. "I repeat. They are walking past house one."

Where are they going next? I wonder. I assumed they would check the closest house.

Will they cross the street to *The Tower*, where Ahmed is watching? They should not be able to get inside *The Tower* without him knowing it. Windows have been nailed shut. Pieces of two-by-fours have been nailed across all entryways, except for the front door, which has three separate bolts. If the intruders try to enter the house, he should know it.

"I lost them," Ahmed says. "They moved behind trees near Gus's house."

A few minutes pass. Not knowing where the abductors are going is frightening. I wonder if I should go back upstairs to keep watch from a higher elevation.

"I see them again!" Ahmed snaps. "Gus! They're walking toward our house. Gus? Are you there?!"

I wait to hear confirmation, but nothing comes. Gus and Ahmed had decided to stay in the same house while we all temporarily vacated our homes and monitor the community. They both recognized there's a slight chance they could transmit an infection; but it's the best way to guard each other. However, with it being Ahmed's turn at *The Tower*, Gus is currently alone, probably sleeping.

"I lost them again," Ahmed says. "They're behind more trees."

I look out my front window, down the road. While the stars provide some light, it's dark. I can't see halfway to *The Tower*. I strain my eyes, trying to scan the darkness for movement; but it's futile.

"I see them," Ahmed says. "Gus! They're definitely headed for our house. Gus! Are you awake?"

I feel a pit in my stomach. Why would they skip the first house? How could they know the first house is empty, but the next one is occupied?

Peter and Zach come down the steps, joining me on the first floor.

"You guys should be hiding," I say. I see a look of fear in their eyes. I'm sure I have it too.

"They're entering!" Ahmed shouts. "Gus! Guuuuus!"

Silence. No response. Is Gus sleeping? Hiding? Knowing him, I wouldn't be surprised if he disregarded the radio as unnecessary when he went to bed.

I know the dangers of exiting my house. Darkness could be concealing animals carrying D63. But how do I not get closer to help if needed? Gus is in danger.

"Peter, stay with Zach."

"No. I'll go with you."

"You can't move fast enough. Get to the basement. Please!" Peter is brave and has saved me more than once; but we've agreed there are some things I can do better given his limp, and sometimes it's better to protect his nephew.

I don't wait for a reply. I'm out the door and sprinting down the road with my rifle. My heart is pounding, knowing I'm running toward the threat. I've faced danger more than once, but I'm never use to it, unsure if I'm living out the final moments of my life.

As I'm getting close to the house Tabitha is staying at, I scan the area for a wolf, bear or mountain lion, anything that could be lurking in the dark. The front door springs open, startling me.

"I'm with you," Tabitha whispers loudly, joining my run.

"Lucy, I'm in position," Ahmed says. I know from our prep time that means he is on the first floor of *The Tower*, ready to engage with our best sniper weapon.

Tabitha and I are halfway down the road, but staying toward the left side of the street, ready to jump to cover if needed.

"The door is open," Ahmed says.

I hear two thumps, that sound like some kind of weapon shot. Not a typical gunshot, but a device launching something. We both immediately stop running, as if unsure if something is coming our way.

"What was that?" I ask.

"I don't know," Tabitha responds between heavy breaths.

I click the radio. "Ahmed. Are you okay?"

"Lucy! I can't see!" Ahmed is shouting. He's clearly panicked. "Some kind of smoke screen! Code two." Those are the words that

Jason M. Jolin

signal someone if being taken and we need to fight. "I repeat. Code two. I'm going outside."

I'm instantly filled with dread. This is happening. They are going to abduct Gus. I can't let them do it. I begin sprinting as fast as I can.

"Lucy wait," I hear behind me.

But I'm not slowing down. I move recklessly, not worrying about any potential danger I could run into. While celestial lights reveal large structures, darkness conceals the rest. A predator could strike at any moment. A Wolf. Wolverine. Fisher Cat. Anything.

A light suddenly flashes on from behind me. It's shaking up and down. Instantly I know it is Tabitha, who is running behind. What is she doing? She's giving away our location, the element of surprise.

I stop and turn; Tabitha is about twenty feet behind. Before I can tell her to turn it off, she has already done so. My guess is she turned her flashlight on because I was losing her.

A gunshot goes off. Instinctively, I crouch. The shot seemed to come from the direction of the van. A second and third gunshot rings through the neighborhood. They sound like the first, coming from the same area.

Tabitha screams out in pain. My heart sinks.

"Tabitha!" I run toward her, trying to keep my head low. It's very dark, but I know directionally where she is. I fear getting shot in the back but in never comes. In a few seconds I arrive and see her lying on the ground. I worry she's been killed.

"Tabitha?" I drop to my knees at her right side. I see her right arm across her body holding her left shoulder.

"Lucy?" her voice is weak. "I'm shot."

"I'm here." I'm relieved she's alive, but I don't know how bad she is injured. Looks like she may have been shot in the shoulder.

Through dim lighting, I see her body shaking and anguish on her face.

I frantically remove my sweatshirt and wrap it around her shoulder where she's wounded. Tabitha cries out in pain.

I hear another gunshot, coming from the same direction. And another shot.

148

I hope Ahmed is okay.

Do I call Peter for help? No. I don't want anyone else outside where bullets are flying.

Do I try to go after Gus or stay with Tabitha? My heart doesn't want to let them get away, but I don't know that I can engage them; and leaving Tabitha could be fatal for her. The scent of her wound could attract wolves.

I worry about standing, putting us at risk if more bullets come. But I decide we need to get inside for medical supplies and away from wild predators.

"Come on Tabitha. Stand up."

"I can't," she answers weakly.

I don't take "no" for an answer. "We have to get out of here." I reach under her arms and yank her but I'm not strong enough to get her to her feet. "Come on Tabitha. You have to try!"

I pull again, and Tabitha puts in some effort to stagger to her feet.

I throw her right arm around my neck to help hold her up. I know she's struggling because she has shifted her weight to brace against me. We begin to stumble toward her house. "Hold my sweatshirt against your shoulder."

Should we try to make it to my house or just go to hers? As we approach Tabitha's house, I hear the crunch of sand. Footsteps. My heart sinks again. I'm not sure where they are coming from. I'm disoriented.

"Lucy?" It's Peter. "What happened?" he asks.

"Tabitha's shot. In the shoulder, I think."

"Let me take her." He doesn't wait for a reply. He picks her up in his arms. His upper body is strong enough to carry her, but he can only move so quickly with his limp. I hold the sweatshirt against her shoulder as he shuffles as fast as possible, moving toward our house. I know we have medical supplies; I'm hoping and praying she can hold on.

"Nooooooo!" I hear Ahmed scream from up the road. "Guuuuus!"

My guess is the abductors have gotten away. Instantly, my heart breaks for Gus; and immediately I feel guilt that someone from my community has been abducted. Could I have done more to help? Should I have done something different? One thing is certain, my community can no longer stay in this area.

CHAPTER

FIFTEEN

I wait at the end of the dock for Dario. He's walking back to finish loading his supplies into one of the catamarans. The air is cold. Despite my flannel jacket, a chill runs through my body. It feels like it could snow at any time.

As Dario approaches, he looks up and sees me waiting. "What is it?" he asks. He stops several feet in front of me, taking deep breaths and resting his hands on his hips.

"I'm making one more trip home," I say. "Bringing Peter and Zach with me."

"Are you sure?" His eyebrows furrow. He looks up at the sun. "It may be dusk by the time you get back." Everyone avoids the outdoors at dusk, given the threat of predators coming out to hunt.

It's the day after Gus was abducted. Tabitha is okay. She was shot in the shoulder, but it seems the bullet went directly through her body. We were able to clean, stitch and bandage both bullet holes.

In talking to Ahmed, we're guessing the abductors have some kind of infra-red technology. How else would they have known to bypass the first house, which was a trap, enter the house Gus was in even with the chair in front of the door, and fire smoke bombs to screen Ahmed from having a clear shot to engage them? It's obvious we can't defend ourselves. We must flee.

It's been a long day. No one slept after the abduction; and we've been scrambling to evacuate. While everyone was devastated Gus was taken, we've been too busy to grieve for him. Everyone made two trips from their home to load supplies on the boats. The carcass from a couple weeks ago has been thoroughly eaten, so there are no longer any predators around that.

There is so much we're leaving behind, including releasing all the farm animals into the wild, except for some young chickens each family is taking. But no one wants to risk staying in our neighborhood, even one more night. The community decided that the limited supplies would be sufficient, and we will explore for new ones. We will sleep in the catamarans tonight while someone keeps watch; and then spend all day tomorrow traveling down the river and searching for a new home.

While we have to do it, I'm anxious about the move. Starting over is going to be difficult, and I'm worried about feeding and protecting my son. Peter and I helped Tabitha carry her supplies, so we weren't able to take everything I wanted; and it's been gnawing at me. We have the minimum needed for survival – weapons, a well-pump, solar-powered batteries, tools, medical supplies, a few days rations, as well as six chickens and a rooster. But we could use more of everything, especially ammunition and solar-powered equipment, which is like gold in this new world.

"We'll move quickly," I tell Dario. "But if for some reason we're not back tonight, don't worry. It means we decided to stay overnight instead of risking it. Don't leave without us – we'll be back in the morning."

I'm not as worried as the rest of the community about staying one more night at our home, as I highly doubt the abductors will come back consecutive days. Based on reports from the other communities, that is not their typical routine. I prefer to get back tonight to be with the community, but I'm not going to risk traveling at dusk.

Dario nods. "Okay. Be careful." He resumes his work. I can tell he's exhausted. I know the feeling; I'm also fatigued.

I step away and begin to head toward Peter and Zach who are sitting against a wall, clearly tired. The wheelbarrow we used to help transport supplies is next to them.

"Lucy?" Tabitha calls.

I turn to my left to see her trying to get to her feet. She's been resting at dock three, clearly isolated from everyone else. I walk over so she doesn't need to exert herself to meet me. I observe the river flowing under the dock and wonder whether the water would freeze if it wasn't moving.

"What is it?" I ask.

"Can I ask you a question about Christians?"

You want to talk about religion, now? I'm thinking. *We need to get out of here. Can't this wait?*

But I bite my tongue and suppress my thoughts. I don't like saying "no" when it comes to the topic of God. "Sure." I say with a nod. I see anguish on her face. I sit down across from her on the dock.

Tabitha speaks softly. "If everything you've told me about God is true...that judgment is real...then I was a few inches away from going to hell...forever."

I don't say anything. I maintain eye contact and press my lips together as a sign of compassion.

"Last night...it really shook me. I mean..." She looks over at the catamarans. "I know everyone is shaken, but I was close to death. Not like getting D63 and coming to terms with dying. It could have been instant death."

I've seen this before. Someone comes close to death, and it wakes them up; it causes them to consider life-after-death. Some people who ignore spiritual truth, become open to it when they face their mortality. Unfortunately, some people don't get a second chance to consider the truth about God and decide their eternal destination.

Tabitha's bottom lip quivers. "Many years ago..." She pauses and nods a couple times. I can tell she's fighting back some emotion. "Many years ago, I wanted to believe in God. I was in my mid-twenties when I started going to a church. A large Christian church. It felt right."

The muscles in her face become tense, revealing her angst. It's obvious this wasn't a good experience.

"I got into a small group and made friends. It was great for a few months, but then I heard things that bothered me. Things I didn't think Christians said. Things I thought were hateful."

Hateful? That's a strong word. I'm not sure what she means, but I already have possibilities running through my mind. There was a time when people accused Christians of being hateful, villainizing them, simply because they disagreed with ideas in the culture. But generally that was wrong. Christians were not being hateful. They disagreed because they cared about people; rather than affirm harmful lies, they desired to share God's truth.

Tabitha has stopped talking, as if expecting me to respond. But I need more information. "What do you mean by hateful?" I ask.

Tabitha stares past me, as if rewatching an event in her mind.

"It was someone I had developed a good relationship with. Someone who I looked up to and told me Christians should love their neighbor. But one night we got into a disagreement. It escalated and she berated me in front of our friends. I was stunned. Maybe hateful is too strong, but she was definitely nasty. I remember immediately thinking, 'Christians are hypocrites'."

Christians are hypocrites? How do I respond to that? Again, Tabitha pauses and eyes me, as if waiting for a response. Obviously, this was personal. Someone hurt her emotionally.

"I'm sorry Tabitha. I'm truly sorry someone hurt you."

Currently, I have mixed emotions. I have genuine sympathy for Tabitha, while I'm also feeling pressed for time, wanting to get to my house for supplies. But I don't want to rush the conversation. I have literally been waiting months to reunite with my friend. Hurrying our discussion would clearly be insensitive.

I'm wondering what to say next. Fortunately, Tabitha interrupts my thoughts.

"I appreciate that Lucy. Really. It did hurt, but it went beyond an argument. It devastated me because I thought I had found something in Christianity. But this feeling of hypocrisy ripped it away. I felt empty. Lost. I decided I would respect everyone's beliefs as true for them, but for me, Christianity was out."

I'm not exactly sure what to say. "I'm glad you told me this. How can I help?"

"I'm thinking about everything we've talked about. A couple

weeks ago, you said it's impossible for all religions to be true. I'm sure you said it before, but it didn't resonate. This time, it rattled my beliefs, and I started thinking a lot about God again. I immediately considered Christianity, like my Mom; but then I remembered this hypocrisy stuff, which just feels like a barrier that I can't get past."

She holds her hand up. "I'm sorry, I know we have bigger things going on, but this is consuming my mind. After last night, I feel urgency to make a decision about God."

It's obvious Tabitha isn't looking for emotional comfort. She wants intellectual reasons. I decide to affirm that there are hypocrites.

"While I would give someone the benefit of the doubt at first, it's possible this person who hurt you wasn't a true Christian. There are people who claim to be Christians, but they're not. While only the Lord knows for sure, people who knowingly, intentionally and continually sin without any remorse are probably not true followers of Jesus. It's probably fair to say they are hypocrites. I don't know if that was this person, but I wouldn't let that stand in the way of you committing to the truth."

"I hear what you are saying, but I don't think that was this person. She really seemed to be a genuine believer." Instantly I regret offering that explanation first. I need to pivot and offer a different response.

"I should have assumed that was the case. Let me offer a couple different reasons I think might help. First, the Bible never says Christians will stop sinning. We desire to follow Jesus and try to refrain from sin, but it still happens. This actually fits with the Christian worldview, that human beings are inclined to sin, which is why we all need a Savior."

Tabitha nods, as if she understands.

"Second, if a Christian does do something that is hypocritical, is that a reflection on Jesus? In other words, just because we mess up, does that mean Christianity is false? Of course not. Even if we mess up, that doesn't change the truth that God exists... that Jesus is the Son of God."

"But don't Christians represent Jesus?" Tabitha asks.

"Yes, but if we do it poorly, that's not a reflection on Him but us, who are fallen. It doesn't mean Christianity is false, it confirms we're not perfect. Do you remember the great musicians and bands we had growing up?"

Tabitha nods.

"If someone who was not a great musician tried to replicate their music but failed, would you blame the great musician? Of course not. You would say the person simply did a bad job. That's the same thing when Christians do a poor job trying to mirror Jesus.[40] When we fail, it doesn't mean Christianity is false; it confirms we need a Savior."

I can see her expression change instantly. It's like a light bulb went on.

"Thank you Lucy." Tabitha nods. "Really. This helps a lot."

It clearly looks like an intellectual barrier has been removed. I'm relieved I didn't refuse her request to chat.

"Great. We can talk more when I get back."

"Get back?" Tabitha asks. Her eyebrows furrow.

"Yeah. I'm doing one more trip. Taking Peter and Zach. I should be back tonight. Or maybe tomorrow morning." With this slight delay, I'm starting to think I might not make it back.

"Tomorrow morning? Aren't you worried they might come back?"

"My preference is to be back tonight, but I'm not overly worried about the abductors coming back right away. It's not their pattern."

Tabitha looks dismayed.

"I…I don't want to wait. Just in case. I feel a burden. I'm ready to become a Christian right now."

I can tell she's nervous, probably from being close to death. But is she serious about this decision?

"This is a big commitment Tabitha. It's the right decision, but are you truly ready to do so?"

"I think so. Yes."

I want to make sure she really knows what she's committing to. "Okay. Let me ask you a few questions. Do you believe God exists?"

"Yeah, I've always believed there's a powerful being that created everything."

"Do you believe you are a sinner? Meaning, you've broken God's moral law."

"That's easy. Of course." She looks down. "I feel guilt. I know I'm not perfect."

"Me too. No one meets God's moral standard. Do you believe Jesus is God, who died for your sins and rose from the dead?"

"Yes."

"Are you willing to put your trust in Jesus? Are you willing to accept Him as Lord, and Savior from your sins?"

I can see Tabitha's eyes fill with tears. One overflows and a tear releases, trickling down her cheek.

"I remember you asking my Mom these things," she says as she wipes her cheek. She nods. "Yes."

I move closer and put my hand on her shoulder. I don't care about D63 right now. I'm overcome with joy. I've been praying for Tabitha for many years. I lead her in a prayer, accepting Jesus as her Lord and Savior.

I can see a weight lifted off her shoulders.

"Tabitha, I can't tell you how happy I am for you. You should take joy in knowing your sins are forgiven and you will be in heaven with God. And see your Mom again."

I can see the emotion in her eyes.

"I need to run home and hopefully make it back."

"Hopefully?"

I get to my feet. "I mean hopefully tonight."

I give a final smile and turn to leave. As I'm walking away, I notice the position of the sun. Am I going to make it home and back here before dusk? It's going to be close.

CHAPTER
SIXTEEN

Peter and I sit at the kitchen table of our home. We're taking a break from what has been a strenuous day, transporting supplies to the catamarans. We're not going to make it back to the marina today to join the others. By the time we were ready with supplies, the sunlight was beginning to recede. We'll sleep here tonight and leave at first light.

Peter chews on some fruit while I sip water. My drink isn't cold, but it's still refreshing for my depleted body. Zach is upstairs getting 'one more thing' from his room.

It's hitting me that this is the last time we'll be here. I notice the fireplace that kept us warm on many cold nights. I see the reclining chair where I held Zach as a small child on countless nights until he fell asleep. Admittedly, it was comforting for me when I agonized over losing my husband.

This isn't just our shelter; it has been our home for all of Zach's life. I know we need to leave, but the nostalgia is hitting me hard. Earlier today, I didn't have time to reflect on memories. Gus had been taken. The community was frantic. We quickly decided to flee the area. It was organized chaos.

But now, I'm sitting here – idle. It's quiet. I can't help but reminisce.

"Mom!" Zach shouts from upstairs. His tone is filled with panic. Instantly, I know something is seriously wrong. I get a heavy pit in my stomach. My brother and I look at each other, as if both dreading the same thing.

"There's headlights!" Zach yells while running down the second-floor hallway. I feel the blood draining from my head. *It can't be! They can't be back!*

Peter and I rush to the living room window, not waiting for Zach to get to us. I see headlights at the far end of our street.

"They're on our road," Peter says. "We should hide."

"How did they get around the trees?" I ask in a bewildered tone.

"It doesn't matter," Peter says. As I stare down the road, he gives my arm a tug. "Lucy. We need to hide."

But I hesitate. I want to see where the vehicle is going. There's nobody else around, so I'm not worried about protecting the community. The community? My anger burns as the raw feelings of Gus being taken re-emerge.

The vehicle isn't stopping. I'm beginning to get nervous, but I can't pull myself away. I'm curious if they're searching for people or scavenging for supplies.

The van continues to travel slowly down our road, halfway to our house.

"Lucy! We should hide," Peter says louder and more sternly. I turn and see Zach standing next to his uncle. I turn back to see the car still proceeding slowly down our road. I recall the possibility of infra-red technology and begin to worry about our safety.

"Okay," I agree. "Head to the basement. I'll be right behind you."

Peter looks at me and nods. I hear them scurry away, as I keep my eyes trained on the approaching vehicle. It hasn't stopped. It's still traveling slowly as if to a destination. Are they headed for our house? Do they somehow know we're here? It's about three-quarters down our road, and fear begins to overtake my curiosity. I need to hide – now!

I move quickly to the basement door and shut it behind me. I click my flashlight on and hurry down the steps. I reach the bottom and turn left, sprinting to the back. I arrive where Peter and Zach are already crouched behind a workbench. It's the best place to watch anyone descending the steps and still be in position to flee the house through the basement door next to us. We previously agreed that this escape plan is a last resort, as someone could be waiting toward the back of the house.

Peter hands me a pistol; one of the weapons we kept down here for emergencies. I assume he has the shotgun. Then I click off the flashlight. It's almost pitch black. There's a small amount of celestial light coming through small basement windows. I can barely see Peter and Zach next to me.

We wait in darkness. The silence is deafening. All I hear, periodically, is our breathing. Seconds turn into minutes.

"Maybe they went to another house," Peter whispers.

"Maybe they left," Zach speaks softly.

"We can't take chances," Peter answers his nephew. "We're going to stay here a long time."

I'm about to speak, when I hear knocking upstairs at the front door. It must be loud for the sound to travel through the floor.

"Shh," I whisper, hushing the conversation.

"Hello?" I faintly hear a female voice, calling loudly from upstairs. "Lucy?"

My heart sinks. Did she call my name? I look at Peter who, as far as I can tell, has a stunned expression. He shakes his head signaling he has no clue how this is possible. I hear the front door upstairs open.

"Lucy?" again, the woman calls my name even louder. She's clearly in the house.

"Lucy don't move," my brother whispers, as if he thinks I'm considering it. I don't know what to think. I'm baffled how she knows my name. There are no records with my name attached to this property. It's perplexing; but I refuse to move.

"Lucy are you here? I know where your husband is."

What? What did she say?!

My eyes grow wide. I feel the blood drain from my head – again! Peter's hand grabs my arm, as if afraid I'm going to run for the steps.

"Mom?" I hear Zach whisper.

"Quiet Zach," Peter whispers. "Nobody move."

How does this person know me? How does she know I had a

husband? She said she knows where he is, as if he is alive. This must be a trap, right? I feel my curiosity rising, beating back my fear.

"Peter let go" I demand.

"Lucy it's a trap."

"How do you know?" I yank my arm away. "Stay here with Zach."

"I'll go. You stay," Peter demands.

"She called for me and mentioned my husband. I'm going." I whisper harshly.

"I'll go with you," Peter offers.

"No. You can't move fast if it's a trap. Please stay with Zach."

He lets out a frustrated sigh but doesn't continue to argue. He's probably stirring with confusion as well. I click my flashlight back on and hasten to the steps. I can hear someone move a chair on the floor above me, at the dining room table. I aim my flashlight and handgun up the steps at the basement door, and slowly begin to ascend the stairs. I step gingerly, trying not to cause the wooden steps to creek.

I know I could be walking into an ambush. This could a sophisticated enemy that somehow knows our weaknesses, dangling a lie to get us to expose ourselves. But how could they know I had a husband who is gone. I can't stop. I must know why she said that.

Still unsure of the possible danger in the house, I continue to approach cautiously, listening for clues for how many people are upstairs. So far, it seems to be only one person. As I'm halfway to the door leading to the first floor, I hear movement around the dining room table and then a set of footsteps leaving that area. They are not careful to be quiet; instead heading for the front of the house.

I strain to listen for any other movement, but it continues to sound like just one person. My extended arms are locked in place, aimed at the door, looking for even the slightest hint of movement by the doorknob.

I hear the front door open and shut. My stomach sinks. Am I losing my opportunity? Will I forever wonder if this person knew my husband? Is this a trap? Did she open and close the door and is actually waiting in the house? Are there others that have silently positioned themselves to ambush me?

I can't take the chance of missing the opportunity to question this person. I rush forward to the basement door, hurry through and dash to the front of the house. As I'm reaching the front, I consider I could be assaulted at any second; but I need to take the chance. I twist the knob and charge through to the outside.

I see the back of a figure turn to face me. A woman. She seems startled. I aim my gun at her.

"Stop," I demand. She has already stopped, but I say it anyway.

"Lucy?" she asks. "Are you Lucy?"

"Don't move!" I order, gun trained on her torso as I slowly take steps toward her. I listen for movement around me, worried about an ambush, but I cannot take my eyes off of her. She is the only possible threat in sight. Her hands rise slowly, a sign of surrender.

"Are you Lucy? I'm here to help."

"Who are you?" I inquire, stopping about fifteen feet from her.

"My name is Rose. You're Lucy, right?"

How does she know me? I'm bewildered. Do I confirm my identity? Is there any risk? Why would abductors be specifically targeting me? I scan her body for weapons but don't see anything obvious.

"I'm not a threat," she shakes her head. "I'm trying to find Lucy." She stands motionless, seemingly genuine. I decide she is not an immediate threat and take a moment to turn right and left looking for danger. Rose looks around as well, apparently wondering what I'm searching for, maybe thinking I have other people with me.

"How do you know me?" I ask. My question admits I'm the one she seeks, but I don't care now. I need information. "How do you know I had a husband?"

"Lucy. Thank goodness," she looks relieved. "I'm not a threat. I'm here to help. Your husband is a prisoner."

My arms begin to shake. I try to fight back the emotion, attempting to stay strong and in control.

"My husband died years ago," I snap, not believing what she is saying. He went missing and I assumed he was killed. It was the only thing that made sense. "Don't lie to me!" I say harshly.

"Lucy, I'm not lying," she shakes her head. "I promise. I'm risking my life coming to you." She seems sincere, but she could be a crafty liar.

"I'm a scientist with a community that has been searching for a cure for D6. We developed a potential cure about five years ago; and Ivan decided to use people for testing. He reasoned that animals couldn't be used for clinical trials given their immunity. I was lied to about the people who were being abducted. I was told we captured stragglers who were about to die, and a few even volunteered for trials. I never spoke to them. I let myself be deceived. Your husband was one of our first prisoners."

My arms begin to tremble violently. I can no longer hold them upright. They begin to drop toward the ground. Is she telling the truth?

"I hated that they experimented on people..." Her head drops as she pauses. "But I convinced myself it was for the sake of humanity. Ultimately, it would be a good thing." Her eyes meet mine again. "Your husband survived testing. He's one of the very few in this world that are immune. Almost everyone else did not survive our trials."

"What does my husband look like?" I interrupt with a skeptic's tone, wanting to believe but testing her story.

"He's about six feet tall, long narrow face, fair complexion, blue eyes," she pauses. "He's okay but has lost a lot of weight since he was taken," she says somberly.

I drop to my knees. It takes everything I have to keep my gun in hand, just-in-case this is still a trap.

"I'm sorry Lucy," Rose offers.

"But how do you know he's my husband?" I want to believe her, but the puzzle is not fitting together.

"We just captured an older man from this community that immediately recognized him in prison. Unfortunately, Ivan witnessed them speaking and had the older man...uh...interrogated."

Gus is obviously the older man that recognized Eli. Now the

puzzle pieces are connecting. I'm horrified and elated at the same time; but more than anything, I'm in shock. My body is going numb.

Rose has stopped talking, as if knowing I need time to chew, swallow, digest and metabolize this information. My mind is spinning, trying to rationalize what I've heard, searching for indications she could be lying.

She said a name. "Who is Ivan?" I ask.

Her face turns downcast. "Ivan leads our community. He's a scientist, who I thought wanted to help people. But when we finalized the cure about six months ago, he decided he wanted to find a way to dilute the cure so that it would only last for one year."

"Why would he do that?" I'm confused.

"Ivan is evil. I have come to realize that. He has convinced everyone this is the right way to bring law and order to human beings. If someone does not follow rules that have been set, they will be ostracized from the community and excluded from annual vaccines. But I know him. He wants to use this vaccine to rule the world. Literally."

Her mouth quivers as she clearly gets choked up. "I can't believe I let myself be deceived all these years." Her hand touches her forehead. "I was foolish. Let myself be convinced by his lies. The past few months I have looked for a way to stop this madness…and… when we captured the older man who recognized your husband, I felt it was a way to get help. I secretly went to him and asked him lots of questions. He trusted me and gave me information that led me to you."

Her empty hands extend to me. "I need your help to free these prisoners. I can't do it alone. I have a plan. I can sneak one person inside the van to assist me. But we need to leave first thing tomorrow morning, or Ivan will be suspicious."

My body feels paralyzed from this news. My husband is alive. There is a cure for this horrific disease. People are being held captive.

"How many people are in prison?" I ask.

"Lucy!" I hear Peter from behind. "What's going on?"

I turn to see Peter step out of the front door, rifle tucked against his shoulder, aimed at Rose. I'm sure this looks precarious to Peter with me am on my knees, as if surrendering to this woman.

"Peter. It's okay!" I assure him. I get to my feet. "She's a friend." Is she? I think so. I hope so.

"How many in prison?" I repeat the question to Rose.

"Four, including your husband and Gus. The rest...were victims of experiments. Will you help me?"

CHAPTER
SEVENTEEN

I study the items on the kitchen table – things I'm bringing with me for this rescue mission. A rifle with twenty bullets. A handgun with three magazines, containing a total of thirty bullets. A folding knife with a four-inch blade. A stun gun, with rechargeable batteries and a solar-powered charging unit. A multi-purpose tool with flat-head and Phillips-head screwdrivers. Heavy-duty wire cutters. Waterproof matches. Stainless steel water canteen. Water-purifying tablets. A spare shirt and socks. Two-days of rations.

I can't think of what else I may need. As much as I have tried to maintain my composure to plan effectively, I'm an emotional wreck. I barely slept last night. The possibility of my husband being alive has left me disoriented.

I begin to place the items in my backpack in the order I think I may need them. Clothes on the bottom. Survival items next. Food and water third. Weapons on top.

"I think she's lying," Peter says from behind, startling me. I'm so engrossed with my thoughts I didn't hear him approach.

Without turning to face him, I continue packing and respond, "That's possible. I know that's possible. Believe me, I'm wrestling with everything." I zip the backpack and turn to face Peter. "But how can I not try?"

I see a look of disappointment on his face, as if he somehow knows this is a bad decision. He presses his lips together and shakes his head. "I don't like it."

"I know there's a chance she's lying," I admit. "I know that. This could be a trap. But I think it's possible she's telling the truth. And if there's a chance Eli is alive..." I feel my emotions exploding inside... again. I cover my mouth with my right hand to keep myself from losing control. A few tears spill out and trickle over my hand. A flood of memories fills my mind. Meeting Eli for the first time in Brazil. "He didn't leave us when we were desperate in Brazil. Remember? He didn't leave me...and I'm not leaving him." I wipe my face and force myself to change my disposition, from anguish to determination.

Peter nods, as if understanding my point and recognizing my decision is a foregone conclusion. Last night I told him this was my intention. We argued for three hours. First Peter was adamant this was a bad idea. Then Peter insisted he be the one to go instead of me. But when Rose showed us the hiding place in one of the van cabinets, there's no way for Peter to fit. I'm the only choice. Besides, it's my husband – I'm going to be the one to go. Now Peter's back to claiming this is a bad idea. He's worried – I get it. But I'm going.

Is it terrifying to leave Zach? Of course. Am I worried about dangers the community could encounter searching for a new home? Yes. But my brother is smart, and I know he will protect Zach with his life. The incident two weeks ago when Zach was lost for a short time, is the only time that has ever happened. And frankly, Zach choosing to become a Christian gives me immeasurable comfort; if something bad does happen, he will go to heaven.

I hear thumping footsteps on the second floor, racing down the hallway. I get a huge pit in my stomach. I'm not ready to say good-bye to my son. I spent all night praying and thinking. Analyzing the situation. In the end, I cannot decline a potential opportunity to rescue my husband. As emotional as this is, I must push forward.

I didn't tell Zach his father may be alive, because I don't know if it's true yet. I don't want to get his hopes up; I'm having a hard enough time myself. I told him I need to leave to try to free some prisoners, which is true. I said it would be dangerous, but I plan to use the smaller boat at the marina that looked functional to meet him and Uncle Peter down the river. The community will set a marker pointing toward the location where I can find them.

I carry my backpack and rifle to the front door, placing both on the floor. Zach bounces down the stairs, stopping a few steps from the bottom at my eye level. His eyes are wide with anticipation. Mine are blurry from tears that have formed. I reach out and grab his hands.

"You know I love you. And this is very hard for me. But I need to leave and see if I can help some people who are prisoners. Uncle Peter will take care of you. I'll find you at our new home as soon as possible."

I study Zach eyes, wondering how much he understands. They're blank. He obviously knows I'm leaving – we talked about that last night; and this is not the first time I've been gone overnight. But this is different; and I'm sure he doesn't fully comprehend I'm purposely walking into a new kind of danger. Either Rose is lying, and I'm headed into an ambush; or she is telling the truth, and I am deliberately going to an unknown place with a kidnapping operation.

"Always remember...there's nothing more important than the truth about God. Nothing. Don't get taken captive by lies about God or who you are. You are valuable and loved." I bite my lip to fight back emotion. "I know this world is scary, but we will all leave this planet someday. Accepting Jesus as your Lord and Savior means you are going to heaven. No matter what happens, hold to that truth and stay committed to Him."

I see Zach's expression turning from a blank stare to a frightened look. I pull him in close and hug him tightly. "I love you so much."

"Love you mom." His words pierce my heart. I feel a tidal wave of emotion welling up inside. I can't keep my composure much longer. I kiss the side of his head and give him one more squeeze.

Pulling away and looking in his eyes one more time, I say, "Be careful and listen to Uncle Peter." I give him a smile and one more kiss, this time on his forehead. I pivot and hug my brother, "Please be safe and protect Zach."

"With my life," Peter responds. "Be careful Lucy."

I release my hug and turn quickly to pick up my backpack and rifle. I open the door and exit the house. I turn back one more time and look at Peter and Zach. "Love you both." They say it back to me as I shut the door.

I turn to the road and see the van at the end of my driveway, lights on, waiting for me. It's daylight, but the sky is gray and filled with clouds. Flurries are falling; and a thin carpet of snow has accumulated on the ground.

I feel my shoulders shaking. It's cold outside, but that's not why I'm quivering. I cover my mouth and pinch my nose hard to restrain my feelings. I force myself to walk away from the house…hoping this is not the last time I will see my brother and son on Earth.

PRINCIPLES OF TRUTH

I hope you enjoyed the story, which will conclude in book three. While the story is a work of fiction, it included important principles about truth. Below is a summary:

1. **DEFINTION: What is truth? Truth is what corresponds to reality.**
    o   Believe it or not, there are multiple theories that attempt to define truth, including three below; however, it's the Correspondence Theory that is reasonable.
        1. *Correspondence Theory*[41]: According to this theory, a statement is true if it corresponds to reality. In other words, a statement or belief is true if it matches the real world or what is factually accurate. This is reasonable.
        2. *Coherence Theory*[42]: According to this theory, a statement is true if it is consistent with other beliefs a person or system maintains. While coherence is important, it is not an adequate definition of truth; just because certain beliefs are consistent within a system, it does not mean the entire system is true. For example, simply because a religion is consistent within its own set of beliefs, that doesn't mean the religion as a whole corresponds to reality.
        3. *Pragmatic Theory*[43]: According to this theory, something is true if it is helpful to a person or society

in accomplishing a task. But again, it is easy to see why this theory is not adequate because a statement could accomplish a goal but not align with reality.

o   Unlike what some people claim, the definition of truth is not based on human opinion. Truth is not simply our perspective or preference, or what we feel is right, or what we believe works for us personally, etc. (see point #5 for further clarification). Any attempt to redefine truth in this way, regardless of the reason, is not only inaccurate, but it could also be harmful and unloving.

2.   **IMPORTANCE: Why should we care about spiritual truth? Our eternal destination is at stake.**

o   We all care about health and safety in this life.

o   Truth is far more important when it comes to our safety regarding eternity.

o   Jesus said that all human beings will be separated between those who will have eternal life and eternal punishment (see below).

1. These will go away into eternal punishment, but the righteous into eternal life. (Matthew 25:46 NASB)

3. **BARRIER #1: Apathy, which is a lack of concern (i.e. indifference), is an enemy for discovering truth.**
   o If you don't care about truth, you won't seek to discover it.
   o Given what is at stake, no one should be apathetic regarding the truth about God.

4. **BARRIER #2: Closed-mindedness is an enemy for discovering truth.**
   o If you are not open to finding truth, you won't discover it.
   o If you're not open to changing your mind (consider other alternatives that could be the truth), you may be a prisoner to a lie.
   o The Apostle Paul wrote about people being taken captive by lies:
      1. See to it that there is no one who takes you *captive through philosophy and empty deception* in accordance with human tradition, in accordance with the elementary principles of the world, rather than in accordance with Christ. (Colossians 2:8 NASB emphasis added).
      2. The Lord's bond-servant must not be quarrelsome, but be kind to all, skillful in teaching, patient when wronged, with gentleness correcting those who are in opposition, if perhaps God may grant them repentance leading to the *knowledge of the truth*, and they may *come to their senses* and escape from the snare of the devil, having been *held captive* by him to do his will. (2 Timothy 2:24-26 NASB emphasis added).

5. **RELATIVISM: Is truth relative (which essentially mean** *all* **truth is based on each person's opinion/perspective)? No – truth is not relative.**
   - o Some truth claims that are subjective and some that are objective, but the idea that all truth is subjective, which is relativism, is not rational.
   - o ✓**SUBJECTIVE TRUTH**: Truth claims are subjective when they are truly based on someone's opinion. For example, the best movie of all time is _____. This is subjective truth because it truly depends on the opinion of each person (the subject). In other words, the truth is dependent on someone's mind.[44]
   - o ✓**OBJECTIVE TRUTH**: Truth claims are objective when they are based on the object, not someone's opinion. For example, "the car is blue" is based on the car (the object), not a person's opinion. In other words, they are independent of someone's mind.[45]
   - o ✗**RELATIVE TRUTH**: This is the concept that all truth is subjective, dependent on a person's mind.[46] In other words, a claim is true if someone accepts it[47] (in other words, it's true for them based on their perspective). Consequently, each person can have their own truth. It's obvious that this does not work, because our opinion cannot change reality. I cannot be correct if I say 1+1=3 from my perspective. Moreover, this concept is self-refuting, because it attempts to make an objective claim about reality that all truth is subjective.[48]
   - o ✓**ABSOLUTE TRUTH**: This is the idea that truth is determined by reality, not a person accepting it; in other words, it is discovered, not created.[49]
     NOTE: Although the concept of 'relative truth' may be popular today because people don't want to offend anyone, it is NOT a rational position. We cannot change truth based on our opinion. I would summarize truth as absolute, whether it is based on a person's opinion

(subjective truth), such as 'Jason like's pizza' or it is not based on a person's opinion (objective truth), such as '1+1=2'.

6. **PLURALISM: It is logically impossible for all religions to be true because they each have core beliefs that contradict, which violates a fundamental law in logic (law of noncontradiction).**
   o "Religious pluralism is the belief that every religion is true."[50]
   o Religious pluralism is impossible because different religions have fundamental beliefs that contradict (e.g. how to go to heaven), which violates the law of noncontradiction.
      1. According to the Law of Non-Contradiction, it is impossible for something to be and not be at the same time and in the same sense.[51]

- What about inclusivism versus exclusivism?
  1. "Inclusivism claims that one religion is explicitly true, while all others are implicitly true."[52]
  2. "Exclusivism is the belief that only one religion is true, and the others opposed to it are false."[53]
- According to the Bible, Christianity is based on exclusivism. In other words, it is explicitly the only true religion. Below are a couple Scripture verses that support this position, first by Jesus and second from the Apostle Peter:
  1. Jesus said to him, "I am the way, and the truth, and the life; no one comes to the Father except through Me. (John 14:6 NASB)
  2. And there is salvation in no one else; for there is no other name under heaven that has been given among mankind by which we must be saved." (Acts 4:12 NASB)

7. **SPIRITUAL TRUTH IS DISCOVERED: We don't decide the truth about God, we discover it.**
   o The truth about God is objective, meaning it is not based on our preference.
   o Unfortunately, many people follow their preference when it comes to God, rather than seek the objective truth.

8. **LOGIC: How do we use reason to discover truth? We use logic, which are the rules for the correct way to reason; and the best explanation for the source of logic is God.**
   o We all use logic, which are rules for the right way to reason.
   o These rules are immaterial, meaning they do not come from the material world.
   o These rules are also objective, meaning they are not based on the opinions of people.
   o Since these rules transcend human opinion but are still necessary for people to be rational, they must come from a source outside of human beings – a divine mind (God).

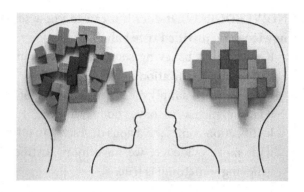

9. **BURDEN OF PROOF: There are three legal definitions for the burden of proof. When it comes to religion with eternity at stake, people should be careful about demanding an unrealistic burden of proof. Fortunately, there is a compelling case for Christianity.**

  o Preponderance of evidence is when a claim is proved to be *more likely true than false*;[54] in other words, more than 50% confidence something is true.

  o Clear and convincing evidence proves a claim is *highly probable*.[55]

  o Beyond a reasonable doubt *leaves a reasonable person without any doubt* something is true.[56]

      1. The confidence level for each of these is approximately 50%, 75% and 90%, respectively.[57]

      2. There is compelling evidence that God exists and Christianity is true. While I cannot put an exact percentage on the confidence level, I believe it is very high.

10. **KNOWLEDGE: What does it mean to know something? Knowledge is "justified true belief."**[58]
   o Knowledge is believing something that is in fact true and having justification for believing it.[59]
   o Being justified simply means we have a right to believe it is true, such as we have good reasons.[60]
   o Justification comes in various degrees.[61] In other words, with more evidence, we have more justification for believing something is true.

11. **BIBLE: Why should we trust the Bible as the source for spiritual truth? Fulfilled prophecy and a unified message from many authors over a long period of time, provide good reasons to believe God inspired the Bible.**
   o The Bible claims to be inspired by God. While this claim does not prove it to be the case (that would be a logical fallacy called 'begging the question') it does clarify what the Bible asserts about the authorship. The Bible verse below supports this claim.

1. *All Scripture is inspired by God* and profitable for teaching, for reproof, for correction, for training in righteousness; so that the man of God may be adequate, equipped for every good work. (2 Timothy 3:16-17 NASB 1995 emphasis added)

o Two reasons to believe God guided the authors, are a unified message and fulfilled prophecy:

1. Unified Message: Although the Bible has diverse authorship (about forty authors over approximately 1500 years[62]), it reveals one central, unified message (salvation for human beings by God descending as a human to die for us – Jesus).

2. Fulfilled Prophecy: The Bible provides hundreds of prophecies that have been fulfilled[63], including prophecies about the Messiah that could not have been recorded after the events.

12. **JESUS: Why should we believe that Jesus is an authoritative source for spiritual truth? There is good historical evidence that Jesus was resurrected, a supernatural miracle validating His claim to be God.**

o   There are a few historical facts that virtually all scholars agree on (even non-Christians); and they are best explained by Jesus's resurrection.

o   We can remember these historical facts with the acronym ACE.

1.   **Appearances**: The disciples claimed the risen Jesus appeared to them.[64] We can believe this for the following reasons:

   ▪   The appearances are written in multiple sources: see the Gospels – Matthew, Mark, Luke and John.[65] Also, the Apostle Paul quoted an early Christian creed that listed appearances by the risen Jesus[66]. (The creed is dated very early, probably within two to eight years after the resurrection."[67])

   ▪   One reason we can believe the appearances truly happened is there are embarrassing details in certain events, which the authors would not have included if they were lying. If they were fabricating the events, they would have portrayed the disciples more favorably.

      ◆   The Bible verse Matthew 28:17, mentions the eleven disciples seeing the risen Jesus and worshiping Him. But it also says that some doubted. I don't believe the author would have said 'some doubted' if he was fabricating the account.

      ◆   Jesus appeared to women before His disciples (Matthew 28:1-10, Mark 16:9, John 20:11-16), which is embarrassing given women witnesses were less credible than men in this region during the 1st century (see Empty Tomb notes below).

- Another reason to believe the written accounts is the disciples were willing to suffer, and even die for these claims.[68] Some people are willing to die for a belief, but the disciples were in position to know whether their belief was true or false, and they would not have been willing to die for a known lie.[69]

2. **Conversions**: Paul, initially an enemy of Christians, was converted after experiencing the risen Jesus. James (the half-brother of Jesus), initially a skeptic, was converted after seeing the risen Jesus.

- Paul
    - Paul was called Saul before He was converted; and he persecuted the Christian church (Acts 8:1-3, Galatians 1:22-23).
    - Paul's conversion is recorded in the Bible, in one of his own letters (Galatians 1:15-16) as well as Luke's account in Acts (Acts 9:1-19; Acts 22:6-16; Acts 26:12-18).
    - We can believe Paul's conversion and claims about Jesus because he was willing to suffer for them, which is recorded in the Bible[70] as well as by early church fathers, such as Polycarp[71] and Clement of Rome.[72] Clement of Rome and Tertullian wrote that Paul died for his faith.[73]
- James
    - James, the half-brother of Jesus, initially did not believe his Brother's claim to be God when He was alive.[74]
    - The Bible records an appearance by the risen Jesus specifically to James, which is recorded in an early creed.[75]
    - Clearly, James became a Christian, as Paul records meeting with James in Jerusalem after his conversion.[76]
    - We can believe James's conversion because he is willing to die for his convictions about Jesus. The Jewish historian Josephus, not a Christian, records that James was stoned to death for his belief.[77]

THE MIRACULOUS CONVERSION OF ST. PAUL.

3. **Empty Tomb**: Jesus's tomb was found empty, as recorded in all four Gospels.[78]
   - We can believe this historical fact for a few reasons: Jerusalem factor, enemy attestation and testimony of women (acronym JET)[79].
     - Jerusalem factor: Jesus was crucified in the same city in which he appeared to His disciples; it would have been impossible for the belief that Jesus rose from the dead if His body was still in the tomb.[80] Therefore, the tomb must have been empty.
     - Enemy attestation: 'E' stands for enemy attestation. Jewish leaders who did not

believe in Jesus, claimed that Jesus's disciples stole His body. This reaction from certain Jews is recorded in the Bible[81] and in a writing from the 2nd century by Justin Martyr.[82] The fact that enemies of Christians said His disciples stole the body, clearly implies the tomb was empty.

- *Testimony of women:* During the first-century, the testimony of Jewish women was considered inferior to a man.[83] Given that, why would all four Gospels record the women being the ones to find the empty tomb? (see footnote 28 for Bible verse references). If the authors were inventing this story about the empty tomb, they almost certainly would have had the men discover the empty tomb to ensure credibility for their claim.

13. **SHARING TRUTH: It is more loving to share spiritual truth than affirm a lie, even if it is difficult for someone to accept; but Christians must share truth with gentleness and respect.**

   o   For Christians, this is a command from the Bible:

1. but sanctify Christ as Lord in your hearts, always being ready to make a defense to everyone who asks you to give an account for the hope that is in you, but *with gentleness and respect;* (1 Peter 3:15 NASB emphasis added)
2. The Lord's bond-servant *must not be quarrelsome,* but be kind to all, skillful in teaching, patient when wronged, *with gentleness correcting those who are in opposition,* if perhaps God may grant them repentance leading to the knowledge of the truth, and they may come to their senses and escape from the snare of the devil, having been held captive by him to do his will. (2 Timothy 2:24-26 NASB emphasis added).

o   Sharing truth with respect is the most effective way in trying to change someone's mind (certainly prayer is most important); people don't respond well to an approach that is aggressive or insulting.

o   Christians need to pray for people and share spiritual truth with the intention to genuinely try to win people, not arguments.

ENDNOTES

1   The movie *A Few Good Men*, was written by Aaron Sorkin, directed by Rob Reiner, produced by Castle Rock Entertainment, released in 1992.

2   This is a point made Dr. Del Tackett in a video series by Focus on the Family: *The Truth Project.*

3   Greg Koukl of Stand-to-Reason, gives a great podcast clarifying these definitions of truth: https://www.str.org/w/what-is-truth?inheritRedirect=true;

4   According to numerous sources, including the source below, truth is what corresponds to reality.

    Norman L Geisler, *Baker Encyclopedia of Christian Apologetics* (Grand Rapids, MI: Baker Academic, 1999), 742.

5   According the source below: "The law of noncontradiction says that [something] cannot be both true and false in the same sense at the same time."

    J.P. Moreland, William Lane Craig, *Philosophical Foundations for a Christian Worldview.* (Downers Grove, IL: InterVarsity Press, 2003), 132.

6   Based on the following source, "Logic is the discipline that studies correct reasoning."

    Davis, Wayne A. Davis, *An Introduction to Logic.* (Englewood Cliffs, NJ: Prentice-Hall, 1986), 1.

7   Bible: Matthew 28:8-10,16-20; Mark 16:9-19; Luke 24:13-31,36-49; John 20:14-23, 26-29; John 21:1-23.

8   Bible: 1 Corinthians 15:3-7

9   Gary R. Habermas, *The Risen Jesus & Future Hope* (Lanham, MD: Rowman & Littlefield, 2003), 17.

10 Some examples from the Bible: Acts 7:54–8:3; Acts 12:1–5; Acts 14:19; Acts 21:30–36; 2 Corinthians 11:24–27.

Also, there is written testimony by early church fathers that support the fact that the apostles were willing to suffer and die for their convictions, including the following examples:

- First Clement 5:2–7—Gary R. Habermas, Michael R. Licona, *The Case for the Resurrection of Jesus*, (Grand Rapids, MI: Kregel Publications, 2004) 57.
- Polycarp 9:1–2— https://www.earlychristianwritings.com/text/polycarp-lightfoot.html
- Ignatius of Antioch—Gary R. Habermas, *The Historical Jesus: Ancient Evidence for the Life of Christ* (Joplin, MO: College Press, 1996), 231–232.
- Tertullian— Habermas and Licona, *The Case for the Resurrection of Jesus*, 58.

11   Norman L. Geisler, Frank Turek. *I Don't Have Enough Faith to Be an Atheist*. Crossway Books: Wheaton, IL © 2004, 294.

12   Bible: Galatians 1:13, 23.

13   Bible: Acts 8:3; 26:9–11.

14   Bible: Acts 9:1–9; 22:6–11; 26:12–18.

15   Bible: Acts 14:19; 2 Corinthians 11:24–27.

16   Polycarp 9:1–2 https://www.earlychristianwritings.com/text/polycarp-lightfoot.html

17   First Clement 5:2–7—Habermas and Licona, *The Case for the Resurrection of Jesus*, 57.

18   First Clement 5:2–7—Habermas and Licona, *The Case for the Resurrection of Jesus*, 57.
      Tertullian— Habermas and Licona, *The Case for the Resurrection of Jesus*, 58.

19   Bible: Mark 3:20-21,31; John 7:2–5.

20   Bible: 1 Corinthians 15:7.

21   Bible: Galatians 1:19.

22   Cited in Josephus's work Antiquities of the Jews 20, as referenced in Michael R. Licona, *The Resurrection of Jesus: A New Historiographical Approach* (Downers Grove, IL: IVP Academic, 2010), 236.

23   Bible: Matthew 28:1–6; Mark 16:1–6; Luke 24:1–3; John 20:1–8.

24   The acronym JET is used by Christian authors and resurrection scholars Gary Habermas and Michael Licona. Each letter stand for "Jerusalem Factor," "Enemy Attestation," and "Testimony of Women." This is cited in the source below:

Gary R. Habermas and Michael R. Licona, *The Case for the Resurrection of Jesus* (Grand Rapids, MI: Kregel, 2004), 70-74.

25　Bible: Matthew 28:11–15.

26　Justin Martyr, in his work *Dialogue with Trypho*, cited a story from Jews regarding the claim that the disciples stole His body. https://www.thegospelcoalition.org/article/4-reasons-to-believe-in-the-empty-tomb/

27　Habermas and Licona, *The Case for the Resurrection of Jesus*, 72.

28　Matthew 28:1-8; Mark 16:1-8; Luke 23:55-24:1-9; John 20:1-3.

29　Habermas and Licona, *The Case for the Resurrection of Jesus*, 44.

30　Greg Koukl wrote an article below refuting the idea that faith is 'wishful thinking'.

　　　https://www.str.org/w/faith-is-not-wishing

　　　Greg Koukl, Christian apologist and author, has written a book called: *Faith is Not Wishing: 13 Essays for Christian Thinkers* (Publisher: Stand to Reason, 2011)

31　Greg Koukl wrote an article below that includes a definition of faith (which is the Greek word *pistis*). "…faith, *pistis*, doesn't mean wishing. It means active trust."

　　　https://www.str.org/w/faith-is-not-wishing

32　Christian apologist Josh McDowell provides a good summary of this point in one of his books: The New Evidence that Demands a Verdict (Nashville, TN: Thomas Nelson, 1999), 4–7.

33　The source below states that religion attempts to answer the five most important questions: Where did we come from? Who are we? Why are we here? How should we live? Where are we going?

　　　Norman L. Geisler, Frank Turek. *I Don't Have Enough Faith to Be an Atheist*. Crossway Books: Wheaton, IL © 2004, 20.

34　Alisa Childers, *Live Your Truth and Other Lies: Exposing Popular Deceptions That Make Us Anxious, Exhausted, and Self-Obsessed* (Carol Stream, IL: Tyndale Momentum, 2022), 2,3.

　　　Alisha mentions that there are multiple ways truth can be manipulated, including christening it with religious language so that people share it without really thinking about it. She also said that lies are easy to accept when they sound beautiful or are mixed with truth.

35　Bible: John 8:31-32 (NASB 2020)

　　　31So Jesus was saying to those Jews who had believed Him, "If you continue in My word, then you are truly My disciples; 32and you will know the truth, and the truth will set you free."

36   According to the source below, our ideas shape the kind of person we become.

J.P. Moreland, William Lane Craig, *Philosophical Foundations for a Christian Worldview*. (Downers Grove, IL: InterVarsity Press, 2003), 11.

37   A good book that teaches how to use questions to effectively maneuver in discussions: Greg Koukl, *Tactics, 10ᵗʰ Anniversary Edition: A Game Plan for Discussing Your Christian Convictions* (Grand Rapids, MI: Zondervan, 2009, 2019)

38   John 14:6 NASB Jesus said to him, "I am the way, and the truth, and the life; no one comes to the Father except through Me.

39   According the source below: "The law of noncontradiction says that [something] cannot be both true and false in the same sense at the same time."

J.P. Moreland, William Lane Craig, *Philosophical Foundations for a Christian Worldview*. (Downers Grove, IL: InterVarsity Press, 2003), 132.

40   This is a reference to Frank Turek's excellent illustration that when someone tries to play Beethoven, yet does it poorly, you don't blame Beethoven but rather the person for not successfully playing it. This is similar to Christians. When we fail to play (or mirror) Jesus and fail, you don't blame Jesus, but rather us.

https://www.youtube.com/watch?v=H5Jfr3X7a94

41   Here are two definitions for the Correspondence Theory of Truth "Truth about reality is what corresponds to the way things really are." Norman L Geisler, Baker Encyclopedia of Christian Apologetics (Grand Rapids, MI: Baker Academic, 1999), 742.

"…a statement is true if and only if what it asserts about a given state of affairs is the case." Ed Hindson, Ergun Caner (General Editors). The Popular Encyclopedia of Apologetics: Surveying the Evidence for the Truth of Christianity (Eugene, OR: Harvest House Publishers, 2008), 479.

42   Here is a definition for the Coherence Theory of Truth "…a given statement is true if it coheres with or does not contradict any other statements that also coheres with each other. Truth is what is internally consistent…Truth is a matter of the internal relations among one's beliefs, not something external to one's system of beliefs." Ed Hindson, Ergun Caner (General Editors). The Popular Encyclopedia

of Apologetics: Surveying the Evidence for the Truth of Christianity (Eugene, OR: Harvest House Publishers, 2008), 480.

43 Here is a definition for the Pragmatic Theory of Truth "...a person's statement is true if it serves some social function or accomplishes some practical utility – that is, if it is workable or useful to one's ends." Ed Hindson, Ergun Caner (General Editors). The Popular Encyclopedia of Apologetics: Surveying the Evidence for the Truth of Christianity (Eugene, OR: Harvest House Publishers, 2008), 481.

44 Greg Koukl of Stand-to-Reason, gives a great podcast clarifying these definitions of truth: https://www.str.org/w/what-is-truth?inheritRedirect=true;

45 Greg Koukl of Stand-to-Reason, gives a great podcast clarifying these definitions of truth: https://www.str.org/w/what-is-truth?inheritRedirect=true;

46 Greg Koukl of Stand-to-Reason, gives a great podcast clarifying these definitions of truth: https://www.str.org/w/what-is-truth?inheritRedirect=true;

47 Below is a quote that supports this point:
    "According to relativism, a claim is true relative to the beliefs or valuations of an individual or group that accepts it. According to relativism, a claim is made true for those who accept it by that very act."
    J.P. Moreland, William Lane Craig, *Philosophical Foundations for a Christian Worldview.* (Downers Grove, IL: InterVarsity Press, 2003), 132.

48 Greg Koukl of Stand-to-Reason, gives a great podcast clarifying these definitions of truth: https://www.str.org/w/what-is-truth?inheritRedirect=true;

49 J.P. Moreland, William Lane Craig, *Philosophical Foundations for a Christian Worldview.* (Downers Grove, IL: InterVarsity Press, 2003), 132.

50 Norman L Geisler, *Baker Encyclopedia of Christian Apologetics* (Grand Rapids, MI: Baker Academic, 1999), 598.

51 Norman L. Geisler, Frank Turek. *I Don't Have Enough Faith to Be an Atheist.* (Wheaton, IL: Crossway Books, 2004), 56.

52 Norman L Geisler, Baker Encyclopedia of Christian Apologetics (Grand Rapids, MI: Baker Academic, 1999), 598.

53 Ibid, 598.

54 According to Cornell Law School website, Preponderance of evidence is defined as follows: "Proving a proposition by the preponderance of

193

the evidence requires demonstrating that the proposition is more likely true than not true."

https://www.law.cornell.edu/wex/preponderance_of_the_evidence#:~:text=Preponderance%20refers%20to%20the%20evidentiary,likely%20true%20than%20not%20true.

55 According to Cornell Law School website, <u>Clear and convincing evidence</u> is defined as follows: "means that the evidence is highly and substantially more likely to be true than untrue. In other words, the fact finder must be convinced that the contention is highly probable." This is based on a reference to the Colorado Supreme Court

https://www.law.cornell.edu/wex/clear_and_convincing_evidence

56 According to Cornell Law School website, <u>Beyond a reasonable doubt</u> is defined as follows: "...there is no other reasonable explanation that can come from the evidence presented..."

https://www.law.cornell.edu/wex/beyond_a_reasonable_doubt

57 According to a Duke Law School article, (*Legal Standards By The Numbers*, by Heidi L. Hansberry, Russell F. Canan, Molly Cannon and Richard Seltzer, Vol.100 No.1 (2016)), the following average percentages were provided in the Conclusion for each burden of proof standard:
- Preponderance of evidence: 54.4%
- Clear and convincing evidence: 73.4%
- Beyond a reasonable doubt: 90.1%

https://judicature.duke.edu/articles/legal-standards-by-the-numbers/

58 J.P. Moreland, William Lane Craig, *Philosophical Foundations for a Christian Worldview.* (Downers Grove, IL: InterVarsity Press, 2003), 74.

59 J.P. Moreland, William Lane Craig, *Philosophical Foundations for a Christian Worldview.* (Downers Grove, IL: InterVarsity Press, 2003), 73-74.

60 Ibid, 76. Quote below form the source:
"If we say a belief is justified, we usually mean that we either have a right to believe it, that we ought to believe it, or that accepting the belief is an intrinsically good, rational thing to do. Often, it is reasonable to take a belief to be true, perhaps because there is good evidence or ground for the belief...:"

61 Ibid, 76.

62 Josh McDowell. *The New Evidence that Demands a Verdict.* (Nashville, TN: Thomas Nelson Publishers, 1999), 4-7.

63 To see some key points on prophecy, as well as some examples, see my website: Christianpoints.com.; and scroll down under the "Points" section.

64 Gary R. Habermas and Michael R. Licona, *The Case for the Resurrection of Jesus* (Grand Rapids, MI: Kregel, 2004), 51.

65 Bible: Matthew 28:8-10,16-20; Mark 16:9-18; Luke 24:13-31,36-49; John 20:14-23, 26-29; John 21:1-23.

66 Bible: 1 Corinthians 15:3-7

67 Gary R. Habermas, *The Risen Jesus & Future Hope* (Lanham, MD: Rowman & Littlefield, 2003), 17.

68 Some examples from the Bible: Acts 7:54–8:3; Acts 12:1–5; Acts 14:19; Acts 21:30–36; 2 Corinthians 11:24–27.

Also, there is written testimony by early church fathers that support the fact that the apostles were willing to suffer and die for their convictions, including the following examples:
- First Clement 5:2–7—Habermas and Licona, *The Case for the Resurrection of Jesus*, 57.
- Polycarp 9:1–2— https://www.earlychristianwritings.com/text/polycarp-lightfoot.html
- Ignatius of Antioch—Gary R. Habermas, *The Historical Jesus: Ancient Evidence for the Life of Christ* (Joplin, MO: College Press, 1996), 231–232.
- Tertullian— Habermas and Licona, *The Case for the Resurrection of Jesus*, 58.

69 Norman L. Geisler, Frank Turek. *I Don't Have Enough Faith to Be an Atheist.* (Wheaton, IL: Crossway Books, 2004), 294.

70 Bible: Acts 14:19; 2 Corinthians 11:24–27.

71 Polycarp 9:1–2 https://www.earlychristianwritings.com/text/polycarp-lightfoot.html

72 First Clement 5:2–7—Gary R. Habermas, Michael R. Licona, *The Case for the Resurrection of Jesus*, (Grand Rapids, MI: Kregel Publications, 2004) 57.

73 First Clement 5:2–7—Habermas and Licona, *The Case for the Resurrection of Jesus*, 57.

Tertullian— Habermas and Licona, *The Case for the Resurrection of Jesus*, 58.

74 Bible: Mark 3:20-21,31; John 7:2-5.

75 Bible: 1 Corinthians 15:7.

76 Bible: Galatians 1:19.

77 Cited in Josephus's work Antiquities of the Jews 20, as referenced in Michael R. Licona, *The Resurrection of Jesus: A New Historiographical Approach* (Downers Grove, IL: IVP Academic, 2010), 236.

78 Bible: Matthew 28:1–6; Mark 16:1–6; Luke 24:1–3; John 20:1–8.

79 Habermas and Licona, *The Case for the Resurrection of Jesus*, 74.

80 William Lane Craig. *Reasonable Faith: Christian Truth and Apologetics.* (Wheaton, IL: Crossway Books, 1984), 276-277.

81 Bible: Matthew 28:11–15.

82 Justin Martyr, in his work *Dialogue with Trypho*, cited a story from Jews regarding the claim that the disciples stole His body. https://www.thegospelcoalition.org/article/4-reasons-to-believe-in-the-empty-tomb/

83 Habermas and Licona, *The Case for the Resurrection of Jesus*, 72.

Printed in the United States
by Baker & Taylor Publisher Services